I0589759

CYNTHIA MELTON

The Wheel

Nightfall, Book One

Cynthia Melton

ISBN: 978-1-0881-4965-2

For Those Who Love A Good Fight.

1

In less than an hour my fate would depend on a spinning wheel. One yank, and my fate sealed.

Anticipation, and an element of fear, trickled through my veins. I peered at my five-foot-two frame and smoothed the skirt of my patched, but clean, yellow dress. My best one, the one with sprigs of blue flowers across the fabric. Not my favorite article of clothing. It made me look younger than my eighteen years.

I couldn't help but hope for a position in a fine house on top of the hill in our community of Soriah where cold didn't seep through holes in the walls and food always graced the table. A job where my private space was more than a cot separated from the rest of the house by a thin blanket hanging from hooks in the ceiling. Crawling through dank leaves in the forest looking for edible plants had long since lost its appeal.

"Crynn Dayholt!" My mother's cry came from the other side of the moth-eaten blanket making up the wall of my bedroom. "You cannot be late today of all days. It's a criminal offense."

Taking a deep breath, I stepped from behind the blanket and sat down to a breakfast of hard biscuits soaking in broth leftover from dinner the night before. "What job do you think I'll get?"

Mam sat across from her. "Maid would be nice, even an assistant in the bakery, working for those rich folks, but you'd have long hours and little free time. You might get a job in one of the factories. It's backbreaking but the hours aren't as long." She leaned her elbows on the table and lowered her voice. A flicker of fear crossed her face. "I've heard there are jobs unimaginable on that board, Crynn. Terrible ones. Pray the wheel doesn't land on one of those. Better to be poor than dead."

The biscuit stuck in my throat. I grabbed for the glass of water next to my battered metal bowl and took a gulp. I, too, had heard rumors of the wheel landing on something, then the applicant disappearing without a trace. What would my disabled mother do if that should happen to me? The small amount of sewing she did whenever she could get her hands on material wouldn't be enough. The rich women on the hill didn't pay much for their tailoring.

I reached across the table. "No matter what, I'll make sure you're taken care of."

She nodded. "I will be, even if you're lost. Lorna's son disappeared. Remember Fawke Newton? His wheel landed on a black square, and he was rushed off right after the feast. Anyway, his mother receives money every month. Not a lot, but enough to live on. She's doing better than we are on my disability, but misses her only son very much."

While I wanted to help better my Mams life, I didn't want to do so at the expense of mine. Outside, one long blare of a siren signaled the time for all eighteen-year-olds to gather at the community hall. I took a deep shuddering breath and pushed to my feet.

Mam grabbed her crutch and forced a smile. "Don't wait for me, dear. You'll be late if you do and that will get you in trouble."

"I love you." I wrapped my arms around her frail body. "I'll see you at the feast."

"God willing."

Her words hovered like a dark shroud over my head. There was nothing exciting about turning the age of an adult. Not in a world made of darkness because of humanity's greed.

Oh, I'd heard tales of a land filled with sunshine and flowers, clean smells and fresh water. Far different from the dark, cold world I'd grown up in. Any light came from fires lit at regular intervals along our cracked streets to keep from freezing. I grabbed a tattered shawl from a hook by the door, wrapped it around my shoulders, and stepped into the frigidness of a summer morning.

"Good day to determine your future, aye Crynn?" A tall lanky boy named Borke slowed his steps to match mine. "I'm hoping to work in the metal factory. With all the destroyed buildings in the lower city, finding work supplies will be a cinch."

"Aren't there…things that live in the cities?" I'd

heard stories told to children to make them behave. Tales of creatures that thrived in the dark. "That would be dangerous."

"Those are fairy tales, Crynn." He scowled. "I bet you'll be a maid in a fancy house. They like the pretty girls to work there. Or," he wiggled his eyebrows, "maybe you'll be an entertainer. I'll be your best customer."

"You shut your mouth right now." I pulled my shawl tighter and shuddered. Entertaining the male species was not something I wanted to consider. Surely the secret powers that be had to be men in order to establish such a career meant only for females.

"Identification, please." A man dressed all in black stood outside the community hall.

I stepped forward and let him scan my pupil. He opened the door and announced my name.

An elderly woman in gray ushered me to a back room away from the tantalizing aromas of roast meat and … was that vegetables? My mouth watered. Only on your eighteenth birthday did you eat like royalty, unless you were one of the rich.

"Wait here until your turn. Applicants are called in alphabetical order. You are toward the front of the nineteen applicants. It won't be long." She left me alone and locked the door behind her.

I glanced around the room barely bigger than a closet and sat on the hard metal chair, the only thing in the room other than myself. I folded my hands in my lap, closed my eyes, and prayed for the perfect future.

My turn came way too soon. The door opened

and the same woman beckoned me to follow her. She stopped in front of a set of double doors. "Through there. March to the front of the room. Do not look to either side or back at me. This is a solemn time. Approach the wheel. You will receive further instructions from the man waiting there."

I nodded and pushed the doors open. No one in the two rows on either side of me glanced my way. From what I could see in front of me, there were maybe twenty people, not counting the five solemn men sitting on a platform next to a giant wheel.

As I approached, I could make out letters in most of the slots of the wheel. One slot was painted a solid red, another a solid black. My throat threatened to seize. What were the jobs those colors represented?

"Stop in the square painted on the floor," a man bellowed from somewhere behind me. "Then raise your right hand."

I stopped and raised my hand.

"Do you swear upon your mother's head that you will accept the fate the wheel chooses for you?"

I nodded.

"Speak up, girl."

"I … do." My voice trembled, betraying my cowardice.

"Spin the wheel."

All sounds ceased as I closed my eyes, gripped the handle, and spun. With hushed whispers the wheel spun around and around until the words and colors blended. I swore those in the room could hear my heart thundering.

The wheel slowed and finally came to a stop. Gasps filled the silence.

I opened my eyes to see the needle firmly in the middle of the black square. My heart stopped, and I glanced over my shoulder at the stricken face of Mams.

"Take your seat," the man ordered.

I rushed forward and practically fell into Mams's lap. She patted my back and muttered over and over that it had to be a mistake. They couldn't take her only child. Except we both knew the wheel never made a mistake. I'd vowed to accept my fate.

I sat in stunned silence as others' needle fell on normal jobs. One young man's fell on the red and he was the only one ordered to spin again. It didn't take a genius to figure out the red was meant only for the females. When all were finished, a smiling man in pristine white robes stood and invited us all to partake in a feast.

"Am I the only one who landed on black?" I asked my mother.

Tears filled her eyes as she nodded. "Only you, the smallest and prettiest." She lifted her chin. "We'll be fine. Wherever you go, you will be fine. I have faith."

Oh, how I wished I shared her faith. I believed in the Supreme Being, I just wasn't so sure He believed in me.

I sat in an empty chair next to Mams and stared at a pile of roasted meat and vegetables. How ironic that hours before I'd been starving, and now I'd lost my appetite. Not knowing what lie before me and, knowing I might need whatever strength I could get, I filled my plate, even folding a meal's worth in my napkin and slipping it into my bodice.

Mams had the same idea and filled my pockets. We were poor, but we were smart, and always tried to be prepared. "I won't be able to see you after the feast," Mams whispered. "Stick this knife in your boot. I wish there was a way for you to take the water gourd. With no knowledge of where you're going, we don't know what you'll need."

"Won't they supply me with those things?" My eyes widened.

"I do not know. Keep your wits about you. Be prepared for anything. Always think before you act or speak." She cupped my cheek. "Make me proud."

"I'm frightened."

"Never reveal that to anyone. Never show fear." She straightened. "You are a Dayholt. Your father worked the mines on the outskirts of the territory before his death. He did not show fear. Not once. Even when the ground closed above his head folks said he stayed strong."

"No fear." I forced the words out in a harsh whisper and focused on the food in front of me. Like a roboton I chewed mouthful after mouthful until my full stomach became uncomfortable.

"Crynn Dayholt, you will come with me." A man with bright red hair stared at me from across the table. "The rest of you follow the man in green."

I stood, clasping my Mams's hand. I gave it a squeeze depicting all the love I held for her in my heart then, without looking back, I marched away.

The man led me to a large room full of weapons and piles of clothing. "You will have thirty minutes to gather what you will need."

"What is my job?" I turned to face him. "How do

I know what to take if I don't know what I'll be doing?"

He smiled without humor, a cruel glint in his dark eyes. "You, my tiny one will be the new leader of the Stalkers. Your predecessor died a few days ago. You, my sweet, will hunt Malignants in the burning recesses of the city." He glanced at his watch. "Time starts now."

2

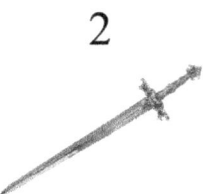

A Stalker? Malignants? I'd never heard

those words before. Did he mean the creatures told in hushed whispers? I stared at shelves of supplies, weapons hanging on hooks, and piles of what I thought was clothes.

I disrobed, tossing my thin yellow dress onto the pile in favor of thicker clothing. I donned some tights and sturdy boots. A leather skirt and jacket lined with fur over a dark tee-shirt. I tied several scarfs around my waist and shoved a pair of tinted goggles onto my head. I stuffed gloves into pockets.

After locating a sturdy canvas bag I could carry on my back, I added the food Mam and I had filched from the feast then approached the shelves of supplies, stuffing as much freeze-dried food and water inside as the bag would hold. How much time did I have left? I dropped a bottle of something called purifying tablets into the bag.

I had no idea how to use any of the weapons

hanging on the wall. I shoved a dagger in each of my boots and slung a scabbard and sword over my shoulder. The door opened as I reached for a white box with a red cross on it. Holding the box behind me, I turned and faced the man who'd locked me in.

His gaze roamed over me. "You don't look like the pretty young thing that came into this room. You actually look the part of a Stalker. Let's hope you last longer than your predecessor."

"I'm still confused as to—"

"It will all be explained." He poked a needle into the flesh of my right forearm. "Your tracker. Follow me. Your orientation starts now. You'll be dropped off in the morning. You might want to put the first aid kit into your pack. You can only leave the room with what you are wearing or is in the backpack. This is a test to your wisdom. I hope you chose well."

My boots slapped against the stone floor as I hurried after my guide. This time, he led me to a room and ordered me to sit in front of a long table. At the other end were three empty chairs. Without a word, he backed from the room and closed the door.

I wasn't sure how much time had passed before another door opened and two men and a woman entered. All were of indeterminate ages and covered with scars. The woman stood close to six-feet tall, the men not much shorter. One man missed an eye, a dark socket where once an eye had been. My fear and apprehension grew.

"She looks rather small," the woman said, her lip curling into a sneer. "If the former leader lasted less than a moon how will this one endure?"

I scowled. "I'm stronger than I look." My legs

might tremble at the thought of my unknown future, but I would not be looked down on by anyone.

"Perhaps. You do seem to have chosen well from the outfitting room." She took her seat between the two men. "Crynn Dayholt, the wheel has chosen you as a Stalker. With the leader having passed, you, being the next chosen, takes his place." She folded her hands and focused a sharp gaze on me. "Question?"

"Why a leader? I'm not even aware of what a Stalker is."

"I'd prefer one of the more experienced Stalkers had taken the position, but they all refused." She set a jar on the table in front of her. "Smear a line of this across each of your cheeks, then put the jar into your bag."

"What is it?"

"The stripes signify you're the leader."

I frowned. "There's something about these stripes the others didn't like, isn't there?"

She shrugged. "You'll find out soon enough."

As I dipped my fingers into the thick paste and painted on the stripes, she continued, "A century ago a plague wiped out most of the human race as I'm sure you learned in your six years of education. Then war and bombs. What was left behind is a world of danger, fire, and bitter cold. Dark days that vary little from the night. A handful of humans survived. Others survived but are not the same. Those are the Malignants, a species intent on our destruction. They eat anything with a heartbeat. The Stalkers have the job of ridding the cities of them so one day mankind can reclaim the lands they lost." Her eyes narrowed.

"This is the most dangerous occupation on the wheel. The three of us were once Stalkers."

That explained the scars. The stripes were a mark. "The Malignants target the leader, don't they?" My blood ran cold.

The man with one eye nodded. "We were all leaders once. If you survive for ten years, you are brought back here to live a life of peace and luxury, such as we can attain."

Somehow, I didn't believe many made it ten years. "Will you train me?"

"You will train tonight, have a few hours of rest, then more training. Day after you'll be dropped in the city." She stood and motioned for me to follow. "When you are in the city, you will have to find food if you run out of the weekly provisions dropped inside the wall. I suggest you make your food and water last. There is little to hunt on the other side of the wall except those creatures."

Realizing her talking was part of my training, I soaked in her words, branding them on my brain. The next room she led me to resembled a wasteland full of discarded metal, bins of burning debris, and steel bars the type used in building. "Is this what the city looks like?"

"In a very small way." She ducked through a door, leaving me alone.

Okay. I turned in a slow circle, freezing as something scraped against the floor. My mouth dried up.

Someone in a hood that obscured their features screamed and rushed me. I scrambled backward falling to the floor. I scuttled backward like a forest crab.

"Stop," a voice called.

I glanced up to see the woman who'd left me there frowning down from behind a glass window.

"You have a sword, don't you? Pull it." She shook her head and withdrew, mumbling I should have chosen a better weapon.

"Idiot girl," the hooded figure hissed. "Try to stay on your feet. Don't worry about hurting me. I'm past harm." He, she, it headed back behind a pile of metal.

Not knowing whether what I faced was human or monster scared me more than the shock of the unexpected attack. Not wanting to be caught unprepared again, I pulled my sword, surprised by its heavy weight. While I struggled to get a tight grip, the next attack came from the back.

Something hit me. I dropped to me knees and dropped the sword. I rolled, pulling a dagger from my boot and thrust upward. The knife slashed through nothing but air. The breath left my body as the hooded figure stood over me. "What are you?"

"A hologram. You did much better. Good instincts. Again." It disappeared.

We trained until I could no longer stay on my feet without fear of falling. "No more, please." I sagged against the wall. I'd either fight well enough to survive or I'd die. At this point, I leaned toward the latter, but still held on to the thin thread of hope that I'd go to sleep and wake up to find it all a dream.

My bed that night was harder than the one I'd slept in at home. A thin blanket all that would cover me. When banging on the door signaled the time to get up, I folded the blanket and shoved it into the pillowcase, tying the case to my pack. Now that I knew I'd be dropped in an unfamiliar, terrifying place and could leave with whatever I could carry, I'd make sure to take it all.

I ignored the humorous look on my trainer's face as I marched past her. She led me into another room where I sat at a table alone. Minutes later, she joined me, setting a plate piled high with meat and doughy biscuits covered with a thick sauce. Other than the feast, I'd never eaten so much.

"Fattening me up?"

"Giving you as much strength as possible before every second is a fight for survival."

"Who are you?" I sopped my biscuit into the sauce, feeling far older than I'd felt the day before.

"Alga. I didn't relish the retired life and while I still eat well and sleep in a soft bed, I wanted to train so no one went in as a Stalker as blind as I did. Not many females are built like me. I wanted to prepare them."

"Why are there no others being trained?"

"No one else had the same ill luck at the wheel as you. Not in a while, at least." She flashed a smile, revealing a mouth with as much missing teeth as there were teeth. "Some years we have more than one, some we have none. We haven't had a new Stalker in almost six months. You'll make number seven to patrol the nearest city."

Great. That means an indeterminate amount had gone before me and perished. Now, only seven against how many Malignants? The food lost its taste and sat in my stomach like a stone. Tears pricked my eyes. I missed Mam and wondered whether I'd ever see her again.

Alga's slap threw my head back. "No tears. Never cry. Do not be weak."

I put a hand to my stinging cheek, the tears flowing freely now. "A warning would have sufficed."

"If you can't handle a slap, you'll not last a week out there."

When she raised her hand again, I reached for the dagger in my right boot. "Don't."

"Good girl." She sat back and laughed. "You'll need that spunk. Now, eat. More training awaits."

I hated her after an hour of sword fight. I wanted to kill her after being chased for two miles by something that might or might not have been another hologram. I wanted to die by the time she led me to my room, minus a blanket and pillowcase this time. No worries. I used the ones I'd stolen and fell into a restless sleep full of faceless monsters.

When Alga woke me the next morning, she again fed me well, with me hiding food on my body when I thought she wasn't looking, then led me up several flights of stairs to the roof. In front of us sat a machine with whirling blades on top. I shot my trainer a wide-eyed look. "Am I expected to get inside that?"

"Yes, and you'll be expected to jump out when told." She jerked her head toward the machine. "Good luck, Crynn. My prayers are with you." She turned and strolled away without a backward glance.

A man with a black mask waved me forward. "Hurry up. I haven't all day."

Struggling to appear brave, I climbed into the

death trap and sat on a hard bench.

"Put that on. You'll need it when you jump out," the pilot said. "See that red handle? You'll pull that before you hit the ground. The chute might come in handy if you need to build shelter. Put that helmet on. You'll be able to hear my commands while wearing it." Before I had it strapped on over my pack and pillowcase, the contraption we rode in rose into the sky.

The landscape under us was one of desolation. Nothing moved past our little district. Other than the hundreds of birds filling the gray sky, we seemed to be the only living things left on the planet. Fires burned around the city, but did little to dispel the gloom. I could only hope the pilot didn't drop me into one.

"See that wall? The Malignants live past there. I'll hover over the first spot I see that isn't swarming with them. There's a map on the wall," the pilot said. "Take it. You'll need it to find your team. When I say jump, take off your helmet and jump or I'll turn and dump you out. Land, fold your chute, and run like hell. Ready?"

When I saw those…things, pale, skinless creatures that ran on two long back legs and two shorter front legs, I wanted to shout no, that I'd never be ready. Instead, I grabbed the map and shoved it down the front of my shirt.

"Go stand by the door."

My hands shook as I undid my seatbelt and staggered toward the opening in the side of the machine. A little way ahead of us, I saw a large, cleared cement area. My guess that it was our target was confirmed within seconds as we hovered over a lot filled with dried weeds.

"You have five seconds to get out of my plane."

I dropped the helmet, took a deep breath, and jumped.

3

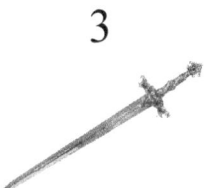

I landed hard. My knees buckled, and I hit the pavement hard enough to knock the breath out of me as if I'd been rammed in the stomach with a board. I'd managed to get the chute open just in time to slow my fall. Trying to ignore the fact those…things were out there, I fought to control my breathing while fighting with a nylon chute intent on keeping me in its cocoon.

By the time I unwrapped myself, the flying machine was gone. Nothing moved. I heard nothing but the wind through the tall weeds and broken buildings. Sitting up slowly, I peered around, then stood, quickly rolling my chute into a tight wad that would fit under my shirt.

The tall buildings cast the day into further darkness, the only light came from fires that still burned after a century. I'd heard tales of the unearthly fires, but had never seen them. They didn't look any different than the one that burned in our hearth at home.

I plunged my hand down the front of my shirt and pulled out the map. It showed the way across the lot I now stood in and through two tall buildings. Then a left, then a right, then another right. I had no idea how I'd know the final place when I reached it and hoped someone would be there to greet me.

A shrill shriek sent me running across the dried grasses. My boots landed with dull thuds on what had once been all concrete, but nature had quickly reclaimed with foliage rising through the cracks. Another shriek came from my right. What if those things waited for me in the shadows? No one would be there to help.

My throat threatened to seize as I pulled my sword and continued as fast and quietly as I could. Things I couldn't see scurried through the weeds. Something clanged ahead of me. I wouldn't be deterred. I increased my pace, staying in the middle of what was once a road and stopped periodically to hunker down behind a hunk of twisted metal to gather my wits and take stock of my surroundings.

My stomach rumbled, reminding me it had been a few hours since I'd eaten. I dug in my back and grabbed a stale biscuit. Not knowing how long until a food drop, I needed to make what I had last as long as possible. Getting to my feet, I walked as I nibbled, my ears strained to hear, and my eyes open to see.

Something darted across the road in front of me. The bite of biscuit stuck in my throat. I covered my mouth and coughed. A shriek sounded again, this time closer. I barely got my sword out before…it…jumped at me. Something pale and pink, half human, half beast, with large fangs, big eyes and ears, and a smell bad enough to knock you over.

I fell backward, sword held upright. The Malignant impaled itself on the sword. Dark blood spilled from its gut. I gagged and rolled away, yanking my weapon free. I kicked the offending creature. "You aren't so bad all on your own." The problem was there was more of them scuttling through the buildings.

A quick glance at the map, and I continued toward my destination. Slow going with piles of debris and ancient vehicles blocking my path. Shadows darted past open windows of buildings long empty of human occupation. I'd never felt lonelier in my life.

Remembering Alga's warning not to cry, I squared my shoulders, blinked back tears, and continued my race toward what I hoped was safety and companionship. I careened around a corner and ran smack into a hard vest-covered chest. Reaching for my sword had become second nature.

"Whoa, there, shrimp." A young bald man with a few days of stubble on his face grabbed my wrist. He looked to be a few years older than myself. "No need to kill me. I think we're on the same side."

I narrowed my eyes and sheathed my sword. "How did you find me?"

"A helicopter is hard to miss." He grinned.

So, that's what it was called. It surprised me that I hadn't seen a photo of one in the books I'd read. "For you and every Malignant within five miles. I'm Crynn Dayholt." I thrust out my hand.

He glanced at my blood-covered hand. "I'll pass

on the shake. Name's Fawke Newton. You're smaller and younger than our last leader, but you've obviously seen action and survived. Follow me."

"Your mother misses you."

Pain flickered across his strong face. "No more than I miss her. I've only two more years and I can be rid of this place, maybe."

"You've been here for eight years?" My eyes widened.

He nodded. "A few of the other Stalkers have been here longer. With a criminal past, they've been assigned this job for the rest of their lives."

"Are there laws out here to break?"

"Yes." His navy eyes settled on me. "Being responsible for the death of another Stalker because of negligence could get you here for life. So can cowardice."

I couldn't help but wonder if those who'd been here a while had done one of those or committed their crimes back home. Time would tell. I vowed not to betray or hinder my teammates.

"The oldest member of our team, Ezra, chose to stay. Said he had nothing left for him back home."

"Where are the others?" My short legs had a hard time keeping up with his longer stride.

"At the shelter. Finding you only took one of us." His gaze raked over me again and he laughed. "You're loaded down, aren't you?"

"I didn't know what I'd need." I hitched my chin at his teasing.

"First thing will be to get you cleaned up. You reek." He fell silent as the sounds through the buildings intensified.

"You've water here?"

"Not to drink until a drop is made." He held up a fist, signaling me to stop. "We'll have to take a short cut. There are too many of them between us and the others." He grabbed me close enough to smear the blood on my chest onto his. "Covering our smell is the best thing. Duck in here."

Why wasn't Fawke the leader? He obviously knew what to do, where to go, how to protect himself. I had so many questions whirling in my head, but the deeper we got into the building the more the instinct to be quiet rose. So did the smell of rot and decay.

I untied a scarf from around my waist and covered my nose and mouth much to Fawke's amusement. His eyes twinkled before he turned and continued the march forward. He could laugh all he wanted, but the smell of myself and the air around us made my stomach churn. If I had a few drops of Mams's precious floral scent I'd have sprinkled some on the scarf. I had a feeling those type of luxuries were far in my future.

Fawke led me through one building after another, stopping to press his back against the wall, let an unseen Malignant pass, then stepping back into the open and continuing. I copied his movements and made note of anything that would show me the way again should I be out alone.

As we walked, I noted how overdressed I seemed in contrast to his camouflage pants and shirt. A dark scarf hung around his neck. Tied to his right thigh was something similar to my sheath but that was not a sword he carried in his hand. It rather looked like a cannon of some kind. The vest I'd smashed my nose against was gray and made of a hard substance, no doubt a shield of some sort. The cold didn't seem to bother him like it did me.

He stopped suddenly, and I ran into the back of him. He sighed and glanced over his shoulder with a scowl. Putting a finger to his lips, he shook his head.

I nodded, my face heating. My legs felt as heavy as boulders from all the walking and running I'd done that day. All I wanted to do was drink something cool and lie down, pretending the last two days was nothing more than a nightmare. But, the cold, the fires, the sounds and smells were all very real.

"See that tunnel?" Fawke pointed to an opening under a building across from us. "That's our shelter. Only one way in and one way out."

"Isn't that a Malignant lying in wait?" I motioned to one lying next to the opening.

"It's dead. It's there to cover our scent so we can come and go, although the blood you're covered with should suffice right now. Come quick and be silent." He sprinted across the open ground and into the tunnel.

Before I could change my mind, I darted after him, skirting around the dead body, and into an inky blackness. After a few seconds my eyes adjusted enough for me to see a glimmer of light shining from the end of the tunnel. Time for me to meet the rest of my comrades.

I hitched my chin, straightened my back, stepped into the light, and stopped. My gaze flicked over the group of six, but I stood silent and let them inspect me.

"Guys, meet our new leader, Crynn Dayholt. She got the lucky winning spin on the wheel." Fawke bowed toward me. "She's already seen action and lived to tell the tale."

"Let's hope it wasn't dumb luck." A man with gray hair cut short, wearing blue denim pants and a leather jacket nodded my way. "I'm Ezra Bruno, long time and life-time Stalker."

A man with ebony skin introduced himself as Dante Pitts. Unless he was one of the criminals, his servitude would be over before Fawke's, judging by his age. Another man not as old as Ezra introduced himself as Moses Rake. A girl a little older than myself was named Gage Blue, and the last member of our group, also female and older than she should have been to still be there identified herself as Kira Darke.

Kira offered to show me where to clean up and led me down a short hall away from the others. Water spilled from a hole above us to disappear into another hole in the floor. "The water's cold as ice," she said, "but it'll get that blood off your clothes. This is where you'll shower when you need to. Just don't drink the stuff. It's bitter, and you'll spend a lot of time on the toilet." She gave me a thin-lipped smile. "Join us when you're done so we can fill you in on things. You sure do wear a lot of clothes."

"Wait. How long have you been here?" I started peeling off my packs and layers.

"Over twelve years, I think." Her shoulders slumped. "Bring any food supplies out with you. We share everything here in order to survive. Hoarding is against the rules."

I almost thought against following that particular request, but realized it could be construed as hindering my comrades and/or putting them in danger. From what I'd seen so far, staying here one minute past my twenty-eighth birthday was one minute too long.

Kira hadn't been joking about the water's temperature. My fingers were numb before I had all the blood scrubbed from my clothes. When I'd finished, I donned my wet things and dragged my packs back to where the others waited.

While they watched, I pulled out the food I'd taken from the feast and breakfast each morning. Appreciation glowed on Fawke's face. I ducked my head to hide my pleasure.

"You believe in being prepared for anything," he said, "as evidenced by food I recognize from years ago and all the things you've carried on your back. Maybe you'll be a worthy leader after all."

I stood and stared at each of the others in turn. "Why didn't one of you take the role of leader? You've more experience than I could gain in two days of training and one day making my way here."

Ezra laughed. "Because those black stripes on your face means the Malignants will target you first."

I reached up and touched the tacky strip on my face.

"To remove that status symbol," Gage said, "means an eternity spent here. None of us wanted that responsibility."

"It appears I got lucky." I sat on a roughly made chair and stared at the fire someone had thoughtfully built. I didn't plan on moving until my clothes dried, and my mind grasped the new reality of my life.

How would anyone know if I wiped away the stripes unless one of my team told? Who would they tell?

4

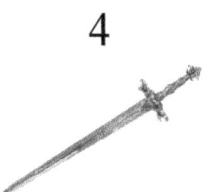

The next morning, I shoved my pillow and blanket into a battered locker Fawke had assigned to me. He assured me no one would take my things, but since I was the only one with something soft for my head, a niggle of doubt plagued me. I didn't know these people I'd been assigned to work with. Without a lock, I had no other option than to trust them. My backpack had grown heavy, and I didn't relish always having it on. When had I grown so pessimistic? When the wheel had landed on that single black square, that's when.

Breakfast that morning consisted of the stale biscuits I turned over to the group and some kind of gray, watery soup. More than I was used to, no matter how unappealing it seemed. "What days do you receive the weekly drop?"

"Sundays at noon," Gage said, cutting the biscuits in half, handing us each a half, then spooning the gravy over the top.

"That's today." I grinned.

"That smile won't last long." Ezra sopped up his gravy. "The Malignants have gotten used to the drop and wait for us to arrive. We have to fight our way to the crate. That's where we keep losing our leader."

It wouldn't happen to me. I summoned up whatever authority I'd been blessed with and stared at each person around the fire. "I'm the leader, right? You have to do as I say, correct?"

Six pairs of eyes narrowed. Six heads nodded reluctantly.

"Good. We'll all wear hoods that cover the bottom half of our faces, leaving only our eyes free. If those things are looking for these black stripes on my cheeks, they won't know which of us has them. We'll all be at the same risk." I crossed my arms. "It appears to me that you haven't been very good protectors of your leader in the past. I plan to remedy that."

Shocked silence greeted me before Moses started laughing. "Girl, you've got balls bigger than Ezra's head. I think I'm going to like you. Heck, yeah, I'll cover my head. I want you around long enough to see what you can actually do. I don't have a lot of faith in someone your age."

Admiration shined from Fawke's eyes, and he winked. "There's some dark fabric around here somewhere. We'll fashion those into some kind of a scarf."

"And," I added. "we all smear some Malignant blood on us before we venture out."

"That's a waste of water to wash off," Kira said, frowning. "Water isn't easy to come by if it doesn't rain."

"All exposed skin will have the blood. The dead one outside keeps them from coming in here. Why wouldn't it work out there? There seems to be a waterfall of the bitter water flowing from above. We'll wash with that." I took my plate away from the others wanting a little time to myself. I didn't know if my plan would work, but I'd try anything to stay alive during my ten years of hell.

When Kira finished eating, she retrieved long strips of tattered fabric and showed us all how to wind them around our heads, hiding everything but our eyes. It wouldn't make breathing easy, but it might keep me alive. I made a small nose slit with my knife.

Dante went out and brought back a rusty metal can full of foul blood. "If this doesn't make you want to die, nothing will."

I immediately regretted cutting a hole for my nose. My stomach rebelled, and I swallowed against the rising nausea.

"Time to go." Fawke said once we'd covered our exposed skin with gunk and fashioned our hoods. He got to his feet and glanced my way, seeming to wait and see if I'd issue an order.

Without speaking, I grabbed my weapons and fell in line. Who was I to question someone who knew the area? I'd already spoken up enough that morning.

Rather than go the way we had the day before, Fawke led us through tunnels deep underground. Cement walls curved over our heads. An iron rail stretched in both directions at our feet. Dirty water dripped down the sides. The only light came from cracks in the surface above us.

"You walk in the middle," Kira said.

"No, as leader, I'll walk behind Fawke." I set my chin. "We're equals now. I won't be any more protected than the rest of you. I'd go ahead if I knew the way."

The others fell back without argument. I ducked my head to hide my smile. I could get used to ushering orders. As the only child, I'd never had anyone to boss around before.

"Don't get too big of a head," Fawke whispered. "They may act obedient, but they'll rebel if they feel strongly enough against something you want."

"I'll remember that."

He put his finger to his lips, silently telling me no more talking.

The sound of scrapes, wails, and grunts came from every dark hole in the wall we passed but nothing charged us. I peered into the blackness, spotting the glow of greenish eyes on occasion. I wanted to ask whether the Malignants and us were really the only living things left in the city.

We'd formed a community of sorts on the other side of the wall. The city looked large and spread out from the sky. What if others had found refuge somewhere, too? Surely, Soriah hadn't been the only survivors of the earth's devastation. When the bombs had exploded, spreading disease and fear, others could have been separated from those left in Soriah. The planet was a big place according to the few books I'd seen.

Fawke stopped and turned left, heading up a set

of rickety metal steps. He held up his fist to stop us, then stepped outside. After a few seconds, he waved us forward.

I squinted against the tepid glare of the pale daylight and pulled the goggles I'd brought with me into place. They'd provide protection from whatever particles the wind stirred up and, hopefully, keep my vision clear for fighting. I swallowed against a dry throat and glanced around.

We'd stepped into a space between tall buildings, something that might have once been pretty with trees and flowers, maybe a water fountain like I'd seen in a book once. A place too small for any flying aircraft to land, though. I didn't think it large enough for a person to jump and land with any accuracy. Overhead, a wooden crate attached to a white chute floated in our direction. The plane that had dropped it already gone.

I pulled my sword from its scabbard. The blood on my face and neck had dried and cracked, making my skin itch. Kira might complain about the use of water, but I had barely any skin showing and could only pray I stunk enough to keep the Malignants away.

The crate landed with a thud. Still nobody moved.

"What are you waiting for?" I whispered.

"I'm wondering whether we'll give up our cover if we take the box. The Malignants have no need for our food and water. They're scavengers, preferring dead over alive. They kill us and let us rot before they feast on our carcass." Fawke shook his head. "Something's wrong. It's too quiet."

"They're confused," Gage said. "They know we should be here, but they can't smell us. We should take the crate and run back into the safety of the tunnels."

"Safety or a trap?" Ezra sneered.

Before we could speculate further, Dante pushed past us, grabbed the box and hefted it on his shoulders. As if on cue, a dozen Malignants sprinted from the buildings around us.

"Don't just stand there!" Dante raced past us. "Run."

We didn't have to be told twice. We turned and ran, our steps thundering down the steel steps and back into the tunnel. Fawke again took the lead, ducking into the first small tunnel that branched off the main one. We stood there, barely breathing, while Malignants milled around just a few feet away. Now that we weren't in sight, we'd confused them again. I couldn't stop a grin from spreading across my face. My plan had worked.

Once our predators gave up and left the tunnel, we slipped from our hiding place and headed home. My steps were lighter than they'd been since spinning that cursed wheel. Maybe I had leadership qualities after all. Me. Crynn Dayholt, barely eighteen-years-old, leader of a group of warriors.

When we arrived at what we called home, I got pats on the back. Even Kira smiled as she handed out wet rags for us to wash with. I knew the Malignants would eventually figure out our ploy, but I'd enjoy the warm feeling of success while I could.

Because of his bravery or stupidity, whichever way one wanted to view his actions, Dante got the privilege of opening the crate. "More water sanitizer." He held up a bottle of silver liquid, his dark eyes settling on me. "Do not drink any water that hasn't been boiled or had three drops of this added, Boss. You'll die very painfully within minutes." His teeth flashed bright against his dark skin.

"I've some tablets in my pack," I offered.

He pulled out foil packets of food and a...chocolate bar? I hadn't enjoyed chocolate since Christmas morning three years ago.

Dante divided it into eight pieces and handed each of us a piece that had turned chalky. "It's old, but it's better than nothing."

I agreed. "You get the extra piece for snatching the crate. Don't act without unanimous agreement again, though. We can't afford to lose a seasoned fighter." I popped the piece of candy into my mouth and closed my eyes as the blissful taste of chocolate filled my mouth. "Where did they find this?"

"Who knows and who cares?" Gage laughed. "Every once in a while we get a little luxury in our crate."

"It has to come from somewhere." I glanced around the group. "There wasn't chocolate at the feast, and that night is the most luxurious event Soriah has."

"I've never thought to question," Ezra said, leaning his back against the wall. "I've been here so long all I care about is surviving from day to day and doing my part to rid the world of Malignants until I die or get lucky enough to be pardoned. Not holding my breath on that one."

"Pardoned? Who has that authority?" I had far too much to learn about the world I lived in.

"Somebody living in the Great Hall. Nobody knows for sure."

I'd thought the Great Hall deserted. The once white mansion had been riddled with fire and bullets or so history said. Children grew up being told it was off limits because of poisonous fumes. "Is there a place on the wheel that sends you there?"

Moses looked at me as if I'd grown a second head. "The red spot. Everyone knows the Great Hall is where the entertainment is."

"Obviously not everyone. We grow up believing it to be a place of death."

"That's for your protection, sweetie." Kira laughed derisively and clapped me on the shoulder. "If you'd been unlucky enough to land on that square, you'd have found out the truth. As pretty as you are, you'd have been very popular."

I curled my nose. "I think I prefer it here."

"You might not if you knew that those in the Great Hall live in luxury with furs and silks. Even the girls that entertain live very well." Fawke smiled.

"How would you know that?"

He shrugged. "Rumors and speculation. Settle back, Crynn. All we do on Sunday is fetch our rations and rest up for the week of fighting we have ahead of us. Maybe do a little sparring. Could you use some practice with that sword?"

"I only had two days of training." I'd killed one Malignant, but would be more confident with training.

Fawke tossed me a stick and got to his feet.

"Let's play." His eyes sparkled over his grin.

I licked my suddenly dry lips and gripped the stick the way Alga had taught me, then took the stance. "Don't hold back."

"Don't worry. I won't." He lunged forward.

I parried, the sound of the sticks clanking together loud in the concrete room. "The Malignant I fought didn't have such style. Fight like you're one of them."

Soon, Fawke darted and leaped, spun and lunged like a dust devil with no rhyme or reason to his actions. My arm ached from defending myself. He gave an unearthly shriek and stopped the stick an inch from my neck. "You're dead."

5

After a week of wandering the city killing Malignants, I decided Ezra had a secret. One he didn't want to share with me. I caught him studying a map he carried when he thought everyone was asleep and drawing an X through sections of the city. The man looked for something.

I quietly turned and headed back to my blankets in the corner. I'd bring up the subject over breakfast the next morning. As leader, I deserved, no needed, to know if we were there for a purpose other than killing Malignants.

"How many Malignants are there?" I asked the next morning over a bowl of watery oatmeal.

"How many humans were there before the bombs fell?" Kira shrugged. "Subtract the humans left and you have the number of Malignants."

"Then the battle we fight is never ending." I lifted the bowl and slurped the last of what remained. "We'll never rid the world of them. What about the other continents? They must be in the same predicament as us. What's the point?" I set my bowl on the floor next to me and stared at Ezra. "I've seen you consulting a map and crossing off sections. What are we really doing here?"

All eyes turned to our oldest member. His lips curled. "You're smart for one so young. Those on the hill don't believe the only survivors are in Soriah. A lookout in the tower has seen living things walking around on two legs and wearing clothes. That is not a Malignant."

"Why haven't you said anything before?" Dante frowned. "Did our former leader know?"

Ezra shook his head. "I was the only one told. As the navigator, those in power felt no one else needed to know."

"So, our excursions are scouting expeditions," I said.

"Exactly."

Fawke pushed to his feet. "I've suspected something to this effect, but with only two years left here, I felt it wise to go along with…whatever."

"If they were friendly, they'd let themselves be known, right?" Gage glanced around the group. "Or are we supposed to determine that after we find them?"

Ezra nodded. "They have to know we're here. Anyone with eyes can see the choppers drop our supplies. I haven't seen any other drops, so we need to assume it's only a matter of time before these others try taking what we have. They may be waiting for us to clear enough creatures out for them to come here."

"Maybe they'll want to team up," I said. "Maybe they're too far away to make contact." Killing Malignants was merely something to do until we accomplished our real mission. The malformed creatures would hinder any real searching we tried to do, thus, they needed to be gotten rid of when we ran across them. It seemed as good a theory as any.

I stood and went to stand in the doorway, stepping over the decaying body of a Malignant. Where would I hide?

"What are you thinking?" Fawke joined me.

"We haven't seen any sign of other humans, which means they aren't hiding close. I'm guessing the lookouts have seen scouts."

"That won't last. If there's a group, they'll venture closer and closer in search of supplies."

I nodded. "Where would they hide outside the city?"

"The outlying sewers, subway tunnels, the mountains?"

"Why hasn't Ezra asked to have home base moved to different sections of the city? Wouldn't that make it easier to locate other survivors? We can only travel so far in a day." I exhaled sharply out of my nose. None of it made sense.

"Without proof, there's no need," Ezra said from behind us. "At the first sign of other survivors, we move. That's my orders. Until we see with our own eyes that there are others, we continue on as we have been."

I whirled. "You take your orders from me, not some unknown on the hill living among luxury. Do you understand?"

He gave me a sardonic salute and stormed away, leaving me thinking I'd made an enemy. The forbidden tears pricked at my eyelids. Being a leader had its drawbacks. As inexperienced as I was, I wouldn't know until any damage was done whether I'd made the right choice.

"Don't worry. Ezra is always gruff. Let's go get this week's supplies." Fawke clapped me on the shoulder.

Which constituted our life. A week of fighting, one day of provisions and rest, then back to a week of fighting. Dread filled me that this would be my life for the next ten years. Spotting a group of Malignants across the weed-filled courtyard, I turned and followed Fawke back into the building.

A few minutes later, armed with our weapons and scarves tied around the lower half of our faces, we headed for the tunnels. My mind drifted to the precious supplies we'd left behind. If there were other survivors, and they found our hideout, they'd clean us out, leaving us with nothing. We needed to find a way to protect our supplies.

"Ezra will fetch the crate this time," I said when we spotted the drop.

"Fine by me." The big man darted forward, grabbed the crate and returned, flashing me a sly grin. "A man's job, not something a tiny girl could accomplish."

He was right, since I'd not be able to carry the weight, but the sarcasm which he said it rankled. Nose in the air, I went to turn, freezing at the sound of Malignants close by. We'd let our guard down and were now surrounded.

Ezra placed the crate on the ground. We formed a circle, backs to the crates, weapons ready, and waited to see whether the creatures would get past the foul smell of us and attack.

Snorts and the sound of calloused feet across concrete grew louder. They sniffed. The growing stench that rose above our own attempt at camouflage alerted us to their closeness.

I fought to regulate my breathing, to keep my heart rate normal. From the sounds around us, I guessed this to be the largest group we'd encountered since my arrival. Had Fawke and I trained enough for me to be an asset?

Gage's breathing next to me came in gasps. "There are too many."

"Shh." Kira shook her head. "Remember your training."

A group of ten Malignants approached at a slow crawl, heads raised, nostrils quivering. They stopped a few feet away, confused by our smell and stillness. One of them opened its mouth and shrieked.

Thank goodness I'd grown used to the sound and didn't move to clamp my hands over my ears. My palm grew sweaty around the handle of my sword. They could see us, or we wouldn't need the scarves to cover the black lines on my face. Humans who smelled like Malignants. How long until they discovered our charade?

They turned and darted away.

"I don't think we'll get away so easily next time." Moses slung his weapon over his shoulder. "The leader studied us a little too long for my taste. Once upon a time, before the bombs and disease, they were like us which means they can think and learn."

Ezra hefted the crate to his shoulder. "Let's get out of here before they come back."

Fawke stopped us at the mouth of the tunnels and listened. Nothing but a sour-smelling breeze came our way. He waved us forward.

Gage's foot sent a rock rolling into a wall.

Shrieks rose around us.

"It's a trap." Dante took off at a sprint, the rest of us on his heels.

I increased my speed at the sound of pursuit to the point I thought my lungs would burst. In order to fight, we needed to be in the open. I glanced back to see Ezra falling behind. The weight of the crate kept him from running at full speed.

"Drop it!"

He shook his head. "We need this."

I slowed, then stopped and turned around. As I did, so did the others. We formed our fighting circle and raised our weapons. "We don't leave anyone behind, and since Ezra is determined not to lose our supplies, we fight. May the Supreme Being be with us." I gave a war cry. The others followed suit.

The approaching creatures faltered in their race toward us. I raised my sword higher and gave another yell. Let them know we wouldn't cower in silence anymore.

The air filled with the sound of weapons firing, lasers slicing through the gloom and cutting the approaching group in half before we had to fight hand-to-hand. I thrust my sword out, slicing a shoulder. The creature screamed and attacked again. Fawke spun, his sword taking off the Malignant's head.

I dropped to one knee and jabbed upward, cutting through the stomach of another. After shooting half of them, taking out the rest was easy, but we weren't safe yet. From down the tunnel came the sounds of many more. "Let's go. Dante, help Ezra."

They each grabbed one of the handles on the crate, and we raced toward our hideout. I gripped the rungs of the ladder that would take me up and out of the tunnel and glanced back. Yellow eyes grew larger as the creatures came closer. I scrambled up the ladder and took a protective stance until the others were safely beside me.

Once they were all up the ladder, we thundered through the building and outside. Keeping to the growing afternoon shadows, we made it to our safe place and dropped in exhausted heaps.

"That was too close," Kira said. "We need a new plan."

"The old one always worked. In and out quietly with each taking turns retrieving the crate." Ezra pried open the lid and frowned. "No more chocolate."

"We need a way to keep our supplies safe in case Ezra is right about other survivors." I propped up on one elbow, too tired to worry about washing off the stench of blood yet. "A hiding place not easily found if someone stumbles across this place."

"We could dig a pit," Moses suggested. "Cover it with something no one would think to move. Something that looks permanent."

I glanced around the room for something to fit his idea. A pit could be easily dug, but finding something to disguise the trap door would be harder.

Concrete blocks, rocks, rusty furniture for decades past. "Dig the pit at the entrance where we keep dead Malignants. No one would dream of moving a decaying corpse to look for supplies."

Fawke grinned. "Great idea, boss. We start digging in the morning."

6

I woke the next morning to rain, something I saw so rarely I couldn't contain my excitement. I rushed to the door and reached out my hand.

"No." Fawke slapped my hand down. "The rain is poison. If it gets on your skin, you grow sick and die."

"Is that how the disease spreads?" The one that had killed most of the world's population and caused some trigger-happy man-in-charge to press the buttons that sent off dozens of nuclear warheads. At least that's what we'd learned in school. Strange how they'd left out the theory of rain spreading the disease.

No one ventured outside in the rain in Soriah either. Not without protective clothing. Work, school, had always been canceled. Going outside was forbidden, but as a child, I hadn't known why.

"We don't think so. Although, not even the Malignants will be out today. We can't turn into one of them. The plague from long ago made them what they are."

I stepped under the building's metal awning and stared across the courtyard. "Do we have gear that's rainproof?"

He narrowed his eyes. "What are you thinking?"

I glanced over my shoulder. "Today is a perfect day to scout. Maybe find the Malignants' lair or a clue to these phantom other survivors."

"No one has ever taken the chance," Kira said, joining us. "A mistake would be fatal."

"I'll take the chance. Do we have the gear or not?"

She nodded. "We received coveralls months ago, masks, gloves, all of it."

I frowned. "None of you thought to test it?" I cut a glance at Fawke.

He shrugged. "I wanted to, but the others said they'd shoot me before letting me back in. Fear is a great deterrent. No one wants to die before returning to Soriah and a life of luxury."

"How often does it rain?"

"Once a month, maybe twice, and it takes days for everything to dry up."

By now, the others had joined us, intrigued, but worried about the track of our conversation. "I'll go," I said. "This could be the perfect time. Soriah wouldn't have sent the equipment if they didn't think it beneficial to us. We're too valuable for them to kill off. I don't think they have the resources to send things that might or might not work."

"We'll all go." Ezra opened a trunk near where he slept.

"No. I'll take Fawke since he knows the area. The rest of you work on the hiding place for our supplies." I waited to see whether Fawke would balk at coming with me.

Instead, a slow grin spread across his face. "Looks like I got the easy job suckers." He snatched a bag from Ezra's hand.

"Those of you digging will need to wear the gear, too," I said. "Just in case. Don't take any chances of splashes hitting your skin or soaking your clothes. Every one of us is needed to fight." I left my furry robe behind, stripped down to my underclothes, and then pulled the thick rubber suit over my clothing and head. A clear mask with holes to breathe through, then tight-fitting rubber gloves completed my outfit. I was covered in rubber from head to toe, same as the others.

Thankfully, the tight-fitting gloves still allowed me to get a good grip on my sword. The Malignants might not go out into the rain, but I planned on us going into buildings in search of where they laid up. We might have to fight our way out.

"I still haven't decided if you're brave or the most insane person I've ever met." Fawke slung his weapon over his shoulder.

"A little of both." Brave? Not even a little bit. I didn't see the point of living in fear, though. I was here for ten years or until I died. Some days, it was a toss up of which I'd prefer.

Gage handed Fawke a bag to hook to his belt. "Food and water. See you before dark." Her eyes searched his. I might be young, but I knew yearning when I saw it.

I sighed and turned away. It wouldn't do to fall for anyone under the circumstances we lived in. Still, my heart dropped a little at the fact Fawke might like someone more than he cared for me.

Taking a deep breath that sounded harsh behind my mask, I stepped into the rain. I waited to see its effect on my suit. The drops rolled like water off a tin roof.

Fawke took the lead across the courtyard. Since that's where we usually spotted the creatures skulking, it seemed a logical choice to me. My feet squelched through the weeds and grass, occasionally sinking into a hole in the concrete. I prayed to the Supreme Being I hadn't made a fatal mistake. The group could survive without me, but they'd die without Fawke's knowledge and experience.

If I'd thought buildings dark before, they were virtually black inside due to the thick curtain of rain. Fawke pointed to a button between my eyes, then pushed his. A flashlight beam shined from his forehead.

I smiled, thinking it merely a piece that helped hold the suit together, and pressed mine. Now that we could see, Fawke continued forward, pulling his sword.

We saw no sign of Malignants on the first floor of the building and climbed iron stairs in a narrow stairwell to the next floor. The door hung on rusty hinges. A cursory glance showed a large, mostly empty room with overturned cabinets, shattered windows, and charred walls. The third floor looked the same. Nothing here.

Down the stairs and to the next building. Even

with the mask the foul air almost choked me. The Malignants had been there, recently.

Fawke motioned me forward, heading in the direction the odor came from. We stepped into a room full of mounds of dried grass in the shapes of large bird nests. While it was obvious the creatures slept here, none were in sight. Keeping against the wall, we continued through the building.

I strained my ears for the slightest sound. It wouldn't come from us unless we brushed up against or rattled something. The rubber soles of our suits made very little noise. The gray of the material blended us into the walls. Someone on the hill had thought through the purpose of the suits. My guess was a former Stalker. For our good or our demise was left to be determined. I had the sinking feeling we were considered very expendable despite my words to the contrary.

Fawke halted us at the rattle of a stone to our right. He motioned his fingers for me to follow him in that direction.

A Malignant squatted in the middle of a room, his nostrils twitching. It never turned its head in our direction.

I smiled. It could see the light, but it couldn't smell us through the rubber. They might have brains, but were too stupid to think this new strange creature in front of them a danger.

I kicked a piece of rubble, sending it crashing into a wall. The creature turned its head in that direction and screamed. I raised my sword and removed its head. I started to ask why we didn't wear the suits every day in our quest to rid the world of the vermin, but the sweat pouring down my back answered me. I removed my mask and lifted my face to a cool, but rancid breeze wafting down a hallway.

Fawke allowed a few seconds before motioning that I put the mask back on. I understood my scent was traceable without every inch of me covered, but I wasn't used to the same discipline and hardships he was.

By mid-day, we'd gone through four of the buildings across the street and only seen the one creature I'd killed. Fawke led me to the top of a building where he bolted a steel door, preventing anything from joining us. A metal awning over a steel box provided us a safe place to sit from the rain.

I removed my mask and pulled the suit from my head. I hadn't felt anything so good in a very long time.

Fawke handed me a canteen. After I drank and handed it back, he handed over a firmly packed protein bar. I grimaced, knowing it would fill my belly and provide necessary nutrients but would taste like dirty cardboard.

I perched on the steel box and took a bite. "Have you had contact with your mother since The Wheel?"

"No. I miss her every day, but it doesn't do me any good to dwell on that fact. I'll see her in two years, if she's still alive. Thank you for letting me know she misses me and is well."

I almost hoped another Stalker would arrive, someone to tell me Mam was well. Homesickness sat heavy in my chest every second since I'd arrived there. Fawke was the closest I could call to a friend in the city, and even that was questionable considering the way Gage had gazed at him. Loneliness was a constant companion. I wasn't sure I could endure ten years of it.

"What happened to your father?"

"He died in the mine. Yours?"

"Same." Most of the men died that way. Mine had fathered me and soon after left my mother a widow with an infant to raise. "Mam is a seamstress working on clothes for the rich, people she never sees. I've seen her run her hands over the silks and satins with a faraway look in her eyes. Sometimes, I dreamed she was one of them who'd been cast out because she'd fallen in love with a poor boy." I laughed without humor. "Childhood fantasies."

"You still dream, Crynn. I hear you sobbing in your sleep." Worry shadowed his features. "Some can't handle the life we live. They snap."

"And die. That won't happen to me."

"I hope not. You've been a smart leader so far. The black tracks on your face are fading."

I touched my cheek. "Will I be punished for not replacing them?"

"I've not read a rule that says you have to replace them if they fade, only that *you* cannot remove them. I think it's a test of some sort." He smiled. "The sweat is helping them to disappear."

I'd be painting them back on as soon as we returned. I wasn't taking any chances of spending the rest of my life here for such a small infraction.

I stood. The rain had stopped. Still, I pulled my hood back up and replaced my mask before stepping to the edge of the roof. Below I could see Dante, Moses, and Ezra digging while the two women worked at putting our supplies into bags and other containers.

Occasionally, a Malignant would skirt along one of the buildings and the group would pause in their work, only to resume when the creature moved on, careful not to touch anything wet. I raised my gaze and froze.

"Fawke, look." I pointed to where a plume of smoke drifted above the faraway mountain. Malignants didn't build fires. The question of more survivors had been answered.

7

"That would take weeks to get to. Most likely months. Hordes of Malignants and who knows what else to get through." Ezra shook his head. "But orders are orders, and we can't deny the fact we aren't alone anymore.

"You're the only one who knows about such orders," Dante said. "How do the rest of us know you aren't leading us from safety into danger for a purpose of your own?"

Ezra's eyes narrowed. "For what reason? I'm a lifer here. What do I care where we go or stay?"

"Finding survivors gives you a chance of escaping this place, doesn't it?" Now that no rain remained on my leather suit, I peeled it off. "These survivors could be rebels against Soriah, am I right?"

"Maybe. My orders weren't very clear." He grabbed a protein bar from a box. "We couldn't leave anytime soon, anyway. It would be stupid to leave all of our supplies behind which means we need a way of transporting them."

"A wagon." Fawke folded his rubber suit. "We could have one built by the time the rain dries."

"Which means we dug a pit for nothing." Dante put an arm over his eyes and fell dramatically back onto his bedding.

"It gave you something to do." I laughed and dressed in my usual clothing of mis-matched pieces scavenged from the room in Soriah. Then, sobering, I asked, "Is there a way to communicate with the leaders of Soriah?"

"I have a radio, but we have a limited amount of calls." Ezra pulled a rectangle box from his pack.

"I think this warrants a call. We need to know what they want us to do. Messing up out here has consequences I don't like." I took the box and set it on a cabinet. "How does it work?"

Ezra fiddled with a knob on the side of the box. A stern-faced woman in black appeared after a few minutes of nothing but a white wall. "Hello, Ezra. It's been a very long time."

I stepped in front of the screen. "I'm Crynn Dayholt, leader of the Stalkers. We've found a plume of smoke rising above a mountain in the distance and want to know our next step."

The woman looked taken aback at my appearance, then gave a cold smile. "Finally, a leader with a backbone. Young, too, I see. I will relay this information to President Cane and get back to you tomorrow." The screen went black.

"President Cane?"

Fawke shrugged. "I've only heard the name a couple of times. He or she is the phantom leader of

Soriah. From what I know, the president never leaves the hill and only a select few have ever seen the president's face."

"Who was the woman we spoke to?" I turned to Ezra.

"Sharon. She's the president's voice. Her words, not mine." He plopped into a cross-legged sitting position. "I haven't spoken to her since the day before I got here, and she gave me that box. She's as old and sour-faced as she was then. Said not to call unless we found other survivors. I really didn't think we would find anyone."

"How many calls do we have?"

"I don't know. She only said a finite number."

It could be that she didn't want Stalkers bothering her. I stepped to the doorway and stared out at an afternoon barely brighter than it had been during the rain. I had no idea how to build a wagon or even how to get out of the city. Other than making decisions I wasn't sure were the right ones to be making, I felt useless.

I turned back to the others. "Can we get what we need to build a wagon without venturing outside?"

"The tunnels and buildings should have what we need." Fawke grabbed a charred piece of wood from the firepit and wrote on the side of a wall. "Six to eight tires, a metal bottom, sides, rope or straps to pull it with…Yeah, we can get this. Do you want to do that today or wait until after we hear from the president?"

"We'll need a way to build a quick shelter," Kira pointed out. "Once we leave the city, we won't have a roof to get under when it rains."

Fawke added shelter to the list. "Some kind of quickly erected tent or we sleep in the wagon. Maybe Soriah will send us one."

"Doesn't hurt to ask when Sharon calls back tomorrow," Ezra said. "They've supplied other things that meant life or death to us. Like the rubber suits."

"Which means our real purpose here isn't to kill Malignants, but to find survivors." I sat on my blankets. "Why? Are these people rebels or were they kicked out of Soriah and left to fend for themselves?"

"If kicked out, then why would Soriah care anymore about them?" Kira opened a can of unidentifiable meat and dumped it into a pot over the fire. "They're way up in the mountains so they can't be of much harm to anyone."

"What if Soriah wants to move back to the city? There are a lot more places for people to reside here once the place is cleaned up." Moses glanced from one face to the other. "There aren't enough eighteen-year-olds landing on black when they spend the wheel. Crynn is the first in years. What if we're to convince the others to help us clear out this place?"

"That would mean they aren't hostile," Gage added.

"None of which we will know until talking to Sharon tomorrow and then finding the other humans." Ezra stretched out. "Wake me when it's time to eat."

I glanced around the large room we called home. Exposed steel beams showed through holes in the walls. A legless table sat propped against a far wall.

That would be perfect for a bottom to our wagon.

With our trackers, Soriah would always know where to send the helicopters to drop our supplies. "Wait a minute." I frowned. "Why haven't they sent one of the helicopters to find these people?"

The others stared at me as if I'd spoken a different language. Ezra opened one eye. "Good question."

What if we were called to dispose of the others? I didn't think I could kill a human. Life was sacred, and the world's population was struggling to increase. Soriah was bursting at the seams, at least in the poor district where I'd grown up. If wanting more bodies to clear out the city was the intentions of the president, then why not change The Wheel by adding more black squares?

No, something far more sinister was behind us finding other survivors. I wrinkled my forehead in thought. "I think the others want nothing to do with Soriah. I think Soriah wants them disposed of to prevent war. Someone is a threat to the president."

Fawke's head whipped to face me. "That's pretty far-fetched."

"Not if you remember your history it isn't. The pride of man has always been his downfall." I smiled, glad I'd paid attention during my years of education. "Resources are precious and few in today's world. What if it's all as simple as Soriah not wanting to share what little is left?"

"That would mean they would want us to dispose of the others." Gage shook her head, stirring the pot. "I couldn't."

Neither could I.

"Disobeying a direct order will get you killed," Kira pointed out. "You won't have a choice."

"We always have a choice." Gage spooned the slop into bowls, handing us each one. "Besides, it's all speculation at this point. Why don't we wait and see what this Sharon says?"

The far-off scream of a Malignant from deep within the building set me on edge. Would I rebel against Soriah given the chance? Would I toss a life of living in fear of Malignants for a more peaceful one in the mountains even if it meant I became a traitor? What if the mountain dwellers lived among demons of their own? Too many questions. No answers.

Fawke watched me, his face clouded with concern as if he could read my thoughts. I took my bowl of food and moved away from the others wanting to be alone with my doubts and questions.

Alone, I ate the tasteless meal that would provide the needed nutrients and energy to accomplish the job I'd been sent to do.

As soon as I woke the next morning, I turned on the radio and waited for Sharon to appear. No one other than Fawke was awake yet, and he sat quietly beside me.

"Miss Dayholt." Sharon's grinning face appeared. "You are an early bird."

"What did President Cane say?"

"He wants the others located. No contact as of yet." Her smiled never faded. "Just the location."

"We'll need a tent that can be erected quickly," I said. "Venturing away from the city will be dangerous."

"I'm sure you can handle things, Miss Dayholt. You seem quite bright."

I stared at her for a moment, then blurted, "Why not send a helicopter to find them?"

Surprise flickered in her eyes. "I told President Cane our young Stalker leader had a good mind." She shrugged. "We sent one helicopter once and it was shot down. We cannot risk that happening again. They are irreplaceable."

"But we're expendable."

She exhaled slowly and nodded.

"What about sending us more fighters?" I tilted my head.

"Not unless they are chosen by The Wheel. You know how things are done here."

I pressed my lips together. "Will we get the tent?"

"You will with Sunday's drop." Her gaze hardened. "Don't try bucking the system, Miss Dayholt. It won't go well for you."

I stiffened at her threat, then nodded and turned off the radio. I glanced over to see Ezra watching. "What did you do to become a lifer?"

"Asked too many questions." He grinned and rolled over. He lied, but I chose to take the warning, at least for now.

"It does seem as if the others don't want anything to do with Soriah," Fawke whispered. "We could very well be going on a suicide mission."

"Yes, but with us dead, there's no one left in this city, which reinforces my idea that the Malignants are not the real reason we're here." I bit my bottom lip. "It doesn't add up." I met his gaze. Could I trust him? I felt as if I could trust all of my group, other than Ezra.

"If our primary purpose was looking for others," Fawke said, nodding, "then why have we remained in this one spot for years? I've lived in this room the entire time I've been here."

"How far out have you ventured?"

"We get a little more ground covered as we clear the area of Malignants, but others trickle back in. The groups we'd meet have fewer now than when I arrived."

I glanced outside. "What draws more in?"

He laughed. "The smell of fresh human meat."

"Which means there will be more and more of the creatures as we get closer to the other survivors." An icy fist gripped my heart.

We would be lambs walking into a blood bath.

8

I gripped my sword, wishing I'd grabbed one of the guns like the others had when I'd been left alone in the supply room. I was the only person without one and would rather shoot than fight a Malignant hand-to-hand. If only the red-haired man had been a little more forthcoming about what I'd actually need in this place. "What happened to the former leader's gun?"

"I have it," Kira said. "I'd only had a sword and knives before he died. Why don't women think of guns instead of swords? The only way to get one now is for one of us to die or you take one from a newbie."

"I grabbed a gun," Gage said, grinning. "Maybe one will drop from the sky."

Us three women stood guard while the men struggled to pile steel bars onto a makeshift carrier. We'd been searching for supplies to make a wagon all day, with little success because of the Malignants. They wanted out of the wet outdoors as much as we did, thus preventing us from scavenging without their constant presence.

A hissing from behind us. Dante swung a bar at the beast's head, caving it in and splattering the other bars with blood and brain matter.

I shuddered. A bloody job, and one I was growing weary of after only a few weeks.

"We've got to get out of here," Fawke said, his voice echoing down the tunnel. "This subway tunnel is too full of them. We're boxed in."

"What about the bars?" Moses hefted one to his shoulder.

"We'll take what we can and find more somewhere else." Fawke grabbed one, Ezra and Dante copying.

We ran as fast as the men could go with their heavy burdens. Climbing the ladders to the upper level proved more challenging. Again, the women stood guard, while the men handed the bars to whoever was at the top of the ladder.

Kira's gun boomed as she fired at the approaching creatures. "We're getting overrun!"

"Drop the bars and go," I ordered, shoving against Moses. "We'll find more. Hurry."

From faraway, I heard the thump of a helicopter. Today wasn't Sunday, which meant they'd either sent our supplies early or were dropping off someone else unlucky enough to be a Stalker. Dropping them off in a field still wet with poison. We had more than one reason to hurry.

Our feet slammed the cracked concrete as we raced through the subway platform, up another set of stairs, and barged into the thankfully empty station.

Moses and Ezra slammed the doors closed and slipped one of the very bars we'd worked so hard to get into the space between the handles.

"If we're to get supplies before the outside dries up, we need to be more vigilant." I leaned against a wall to catch my breath. "We also need to find out what the helicopter is dropping."

Fawke nodded. "I know a place we can see from." He led us up another flight of stairs, then another until we reached a roof.

Bright against the gray sky was the white of a parachute. Attached to that parachute was a person.

"What now? If the wet is poison, we can't let that person sicken and die?" I glanced at the others. "We need everyone." I paced the rooftop, my brain struggling to come up with a plan. How long until the rain was no longer poison? I stopped and took a deep breath. "All we can do is hope the person is wearing a suit. Fawke, come with me. We'll have to get dressed and go get them." Or leave them to survive on their own if they were wet. Considering Soriah knows the danger we'll be heading into in a few days, I bet on the new arrival wearing a suit. The longer I was here, the more I realized how sharp an eye Soriah kept on us Stalkers, but I hadn't figured out how.

We headed back to the ground floor and quickly made our way "home". Fawke and I donned our rubber suits and ventured outside, heading to where new Stalkers were dropped. I wondered why they were dropped so far away when supplies landed in the courtyard outside the building we lived in and said so.

"It's part of the training. If you can't make it through a portion of the city not crawling with hordes of Malignants, then you shouldn't be here."

"None of us should be here." I kicked a rock in my path and sent it clattering.

"Yet we are." He took my hand.

Even though I couldn't feel his touch through the suit, tingles shot up my arm. "Make the best of it then?" I smiled.

"Yep. There." He directed my attention to where someone sprinted toward us, two Malignants on his tail.

The young man wore a leather suit and carried two guns. "I can't shoot with a gun in each hand," he gave a nervous laugh and handed me one. "I got a little greedy when they let me loose in that room. Then a very tall woman told me to give one to the leader. Said that person hadn't been smart enough to grab one." His grin turned cocky.

"Just point and pull the trigger," Fawke said, handing one of the guns to me. "This is the leader."

I sheathed my sword and took aim at one of the Malignants. I lined up the red dot where the thing's heart was and dropped the creature like a rock while Fawke took care of the other one. I knew the feeling of taking what a person could carry. I'd weighed myself down so much, running had often been difficult.

Once the creatures were dead, I turned and offered my hand. "I'm Crynn Dayholt. Leader. Thank you for the weapon. This is Fawke Newton."

"Thanks for the help." He returned the shake. "Jolt Hirsch, newly turned eighteen. I have a feeling

I'm going to hate that needle landing on black. I didn't choose this suit, but was ordered to put it on. Were those Malignants?"

"Yes, and I guarantee you'll regret the choice the wheel made for you. The suit is to protect you from the rain which is poison. Follow us and keep your eyes open."

As we traveled, Fawke filled the newcomer in on life in the city and our primary goal of finding other survivors. "You make number eight in our group."

"That's all?" Jolt's steps faltered. "I'd hoped for more when they told me the job I'd been chosen for. Oh, and Alga said she's surprised to find you still alive."

The temptation to offer him the role of leader tugged at me, but I couldn't. I wouldn't feel right handing something to someone I wasn't willing to bear myself. "I'm as surprised as she is."

"Don't let her size fool you," Fawke said. "Our leader is fearless and bright."

I straightened at the compliment. "We should stop talking. Malignants know a helicopter means a human is around somewhere. They can't smell us, but they can still hear." I left out the fact they seemed to be getting smarter.

Once we arrived home and introductions were made, Jolt emptied the large pack on his back. "I wasn't sure what we needed, so grabbed some tools, food, a sword and knife, and a blanket."

"You'll be glad of the blanket." Moses clapped him on the back. "We'll be glad of the rest. Where's your parachute? They're useful covering out here."

"I cut the lines and ran."

"He was being chased by two Malignants." I propped the gun against the wall. "I'm very grateful that you didn't drop one of the weapons."

"No way. Alga told me to definitely not take only a sword and if my leader was to make it long enough to get home, she'd need the gun.."

I laughed and ducked my head, again wishing the man who'd led me to the room had been as helpful. "We're trying to build a couple of wagons in order to carry our supplies to the mountain, but keep getting set upon by Malignants."

Ezra sorted the food, exclaiming over a pear. "Where did this beauty come from? Fruit is rare indeed."

"Didn't know what it was. It was on a shelf. Looked good, so I took it." Jolt shrugged. His gaze kept flicking to Gage, who blushed. "The hill?"

"I don't care where it came from," Kira said. "Cut it into eights."

"I wasn't the only one who landed on black," Jolt said as we enjoyed the fruit. "There was another guy."

"What happened to him?" Dante asked, biting into his slice of the fruit. "Man, that's good."

"I don't know, but I caught a glimpse of him after the supply room and all he had with him was a knife. The next morning, there were several people in his room." A shadow crossed his features. "I think he killed himself rather than come here."

"Are the people in Soriah familiar with Malignants?" Fawke wiped his fingers on his pants. "I had no idea what they were until my training."

"I don't know. What's up with the continuous

fires burning?"

"Gas mains," Ezra said. "Be glad of them. If you think it's cold and dark now, imagine what life without them would be like."

"I saw another man and woman being led in chains. I think they tried to steal food." Jolt licked the pear juice from his fingers. "Do you think they'll be sent here?"

"The non-violent criminals usually are," Ezra said. "We turn violent real fast once we get here, though."

"Where do the violent ones go?" I asked. "How do they know someone sent here doesn't go rogue and kill the others in order to keep the supplies all to themselves?"

Ezra's laugh lacked humor. "They put a tracker in you, right? If they think you're disposable, all they have to do is punch in a code and that tracker will dislodge and race through your bloodstream straight to your heart. Bucking the system is suicide."

I glanced at the small bump under the skin on my right forearm. It would be a quick death, most likely painless. But, I wasn't a criminal. In ten years, I'd be living a life of luxury with plenty of food and fine clothes. Still young enough to get married and have a family. I wanted to live.

"How many have come and gone since you've been here, Ezra?"

"They were here before me, and they'll be here after me. When I showed up, there were twenty of us. A few were terminated, the others killed by Malignants, we thought." He inhaled sharply through his nose. "I was told that the Stalkers once lived on the outskirts of the city, closer to the mountain, but moved further inland with each death. I'm thinking not all the deaths can be blamed on those creatures."

"Which means the other survivors aren't friendly."

His gaze clashed with mine. "Hence the lack of motivation in hunting them down. Until now. Something must have happened for the President to want them located."

"Now, we're being honest." I moved to my bedding. "Best get some rest. Tomorrow, we go outside in our suits to find what we need for the wagons. No more dark tunnels."

Wrapping my wool blanket around me, I rolled over and faced the wall. Getting Ezra to be truthful was like pulling teeth from one of the Malignants. Almost impossible. We all knew he was a lifer. We all knew he'd been given orders to find survivors and bide his time until orders came for our group to actually start searching. That time had come.

The sight of the smoke was what he'd feared. I still didn't trust him, although I doubted he held anymore secrets. Friendly or not, we'd been given an order to find the others. That didn't mean we had to make contact. If we could live among the Malignants, we could live on the outskirts undetected.

We'd find a way.

9

I lay on my back staring through the gloom at the sagging ceiling as the rest of my group continued to sleep. How did Soriah know what we did or didn't do? Did Ezra communicate with them in some way? Was he a spy for those on the hill or simply a life-long Stalker with nothing to lose?

When it became evident I'd get no more sleep, I sat up and listened to the strangely soothing sounds of those around me snoring. The Malignants must sleep, too, because nights were void of their screams. What if we chose to move at night rather than in the dim light of day? Our rubber helmets had flashlights. We could move faster without having to stop and fight every hour.

"Can't sleep?" Fawks leaned on his right elbow.

I wrapped my arms around my bent knees. "I know we have trackers in our arms. Obviously, they can eliminate us, but my question is…how does Soriah keep tabs on us? I haven't noticed any cameras or recording devices."

"That's a very good question." He moved to a cross-legged sitting position and glanced to where the others slept. "I've wondered about Ezra being a snitch."

"Yeah, but why? Would it shorten his time here? I haven't noticed him receiving any gifts." As leader, I felt it my duty to get to bottom of how we were being watched. "It's far more than our trackers. It's also more than clearing the city of Malignants. That's an impossible task. Maybe that's what a Stalkers purpose was at first, but I think our primary mission has changed."

He scooted closer and lowered his voice. "Be careful. I agree that there is a spy in our midst. Maybe it's Ezra, but it could be someone else."

I faced him. "Can I trust you?"

"Don't trust anyone. Everyone has a price out here. If they're offered the chance to do something to gain their freedom, they will."

"But how?" My shoulders slumped. "How would they be approached?" So many things didn't make sense.

"Weren't you given special instructions before coming here?" He whispered.

"No." I widened my eyes.

"Then, you're lucky. I assumed everyone got their own special assignment. Something to do for Soriah when the time was right."

"What's yours?"

His teeth flashed. "Ah, if I told you, I'd have to kill you."

"What do you get out of it?" Why wasn't I given

a special assignment?

"Extra luxuries when my time here is done." He got up and rolled up his blanket. "Time to get these bums up. We've a lot of scavenging to do if we're going to build two wagons, one big enough for all of us to sleep on."

I got up and straightened my own bedding. "Hopefully, we'll get the tent or something else to keep us from the rain while we sleep." What we needed almost as bad was more Stalkers. "Pulling two wagons through the kind of debris we'll encounter will be rough."

"There's too many supplies for us to carry on our backs. Dropping a trailer when we're attacked will be easier than shucking packs."

I agreed, just wished for an easier way. I nudged Gage with my foot. "Time to feed everyone so we can get started."

Fawke made the rounds of waking everyone else. Our shelter filled with groans.

"Let Kira make breakfast," Gage whined.

"It's your job." I frowned. "Kira will be helping us find supplies. Be glad for the easier task. I'll leave Jolt behind with you to guard our supplies."

"Suits me," the new guy said. "I'm not in any hurry to face those things again. Especially when the other alternative is time with a pretty girl. You can't have been here long, Gage."

"A year." She filled a pot with water running from a hole in the roof, then started a fire. "It's a can of mystery soup again."

I grimaced. "It'll be hot and filling, if nothing else." I longed for one of my mother's biscuits or simple butter sandwiches.

The device propped on a cinderblock crackled. Ezra reached up and turned it on. "Sharon."

"Miss Dayholt, please."

He glowered. "Guess I've been relegated to somewhere below you in the communication pyramid." He gave a sarcastic wave forward.

"Sharon." I stood and awaited instruction.

"We'll be dropping the tent off tomorrow with two thieves delegated to join your ranks. Once you leave the place you've camped for so long, we'll make your weekly drops according to the location of your tracker."

"My tracker?"

Sharon raised a brow. "You are the leader, are you not? If you are to find yourself separated, you'll need what's in that drop. If the others want to partake of these things, they need to keep you safe, don't they?" She clicked off.

I narrowed my eyes and stared at the dark screen. After a second, I touched it. My fingertip connected with the reflection. No space in between. I smiled. I'd discovered how Soriah watched us. At least when we were at camp. Still smiling and deciding to keep the information to myself for now, I moved to the entrance and stared into a gray day finally dry from the rain. Gathering supplies would be cooler without having to wear the suits. Covering our skin with blood would suffice.

Fawke joined me. "What's on your mind?"

"How do you feel about traveling at night? The Malignants sleep."

"It'll be rough. If we wake them, we won't see

them coming? If we sleep during the day, they could sneak up on us."

I exhaled heavily. "I guess we take our chances during the day." I turned and sat by the fire to await breakfast.

After we ate, we spread blood from a recent Malignant we'd killed on our skin. Outside the door, to the right, we had quite the pile of Malignant carcasses. Since we needed to disguise our scent, we consistently dragged a new body to lay over our supplies and block our door. I couldn't believe the smell started to become normal. So did the drab scenery of toppled buildings and eternally burning fires.

I glanced at the sky, recalling a picture from a book of what had once been a bright blue with fluffy white clouds. That seemed like a fairy tale. My parents hadn't even been born when the world ended. I didn't think their parents had either. This was humankinds reality now.

Kira and I marched behind the men as we looked for what we needed. Our job was to guard while they had the laborious task of rolling iron wheels back to camp. Over and over we went, retracing our steps, venturing farther out seeking what we needed.

So far, we hadn't run across enough Malignants to worry about. We'd see them skirting the edges of the shadows, not paying us much attention. Such a needless existence. "What do they eat with the only humans around being us?"

"Rats."

"What?" Kira shot me a glance.

"The Malignants spend their time hunting rats."

She shrugged. "If they can't get a human, yeah, I guess. Never thought about it. Trying not to get eaten myself takes up my time."

I wondered what her special assignment was. I figured I knew Ezra's. Find other survivors. Maybe the others had the same mission, not knowing everyone had been given the same orders. Everyone but me. What did Soriah want me to do? It didn't make sense that they thought a petite eighteen-year-old could do what the previous leader couldn't.

"Am I really the leader because I got the black wheel when there was a vacancy for leader?"

"Yep." She grinned. "Lucky you."

"Why not let the group vote on a leader? Fawke is more qualified."

"Who knows what those crazy rich people who make the rules want. I think it's because he's too valuable to be in such an expendable position. Strong men are needed. Especially those who are good fighters, and he's one of the best. Plus, he has a way of memorizing this city in a way I've not seen anyone else do."

"What about Ezra or Moses?"

"Again, seasoned fighters. Our previous leader was a woman, too. A lifer like Kira, killed on a supply drop." Her features saddened. "I think she let herself be killed on purpose. At thirty-two, she had a very long time left here."

I could see people losing hope. At least life in Soriah, no matter how sparce food and lodging, a person didn't worry about things from your nightmares trying to kill you. Stores carried meager choices of groceries for those with a few coins in their pockets. Here, we waited on the charity of the city who'd sent us here. What would happen to us if they decided to stop the weekly drops?

It took half a day to gather ten iron wheel rims from discarded, rusty vehicles. Finding enough, close by, of the same size proved harder than originally thought.

"Now, we need a bed and more bars to attach the bed, too." Moses surveyed a line of vehicles in front of a towering structure that looked ready to fall at any time. "Something flat."

"The beds of old trucks," Dante said. "We might have to screw two or three together for the larger trailer, but it'll work."

Moses pulled a screwdriver and mallet from his pack. "Let's make some noise. Gals, watch out backs."

"I'll watch with the girls," Fawke said after the first ring of metal against metal.

If nothing drew the Malignants out before the hammering, nothing would. I kept my eyes and ears peeled for any sign of an attack. Blood covering us or not, they'd know we weren't Malignants now.

"Incoming." Kira jerked her chin in the direction we'd come. "Looks like six or eight of them. They're coming in fast."

I raised my gun, setting the sight on one of the creature's head. A deep breath, count to three, release, and squeeze the trigger. The others didn't falter as their comrade fell.

Their hungry shrieks filled the air. Fawke and Kira fired, bringing down two more.

I didn't get my gun up again before an attack

came from my left. The Malignant knocked me on my back, it's snarling teeth snapping mere inches from my neck. I fought to keep my weapon between it and me.

Fawke slammed the barrel of his gun into the creature's skull, then stabbed his knife in the base of its skull. "Are you hurt?"

"No." I scrambled to my feet and pulled my sword, dropping my gun which was no good in hand-to-hand combat. "Ezra, come help. Dante and Moses keep working."

The four of us made quick work of the remaining Malignants. We'd have to hurry, though. More would be coming. We couldn't unscrew rusty metal without making a lot of noise.

It didn't take long for the next group to arrive, this time from the back. Fawke stepped in front of me, shoving me out of the way.

I frowned and moved back to his side. "Backs together, protect Dante and Moses."

The longer we fought, the more apparent it became that Fawke spent more time trying to get between me and one of our attackers then I thought necessary. I'd proven myself a good fighter. "Whatever it is you're up to," I said, taking the head off the last one, "stop it right now. Don't put yourself in danger to protect me." My face heated. "I've told you we're all equal in this group. Unless..." I narrowed my eyes. "I'm your special assignment? Am I right? Because if I am, what good does it do now? You failed at keeping the prior leader alive. Let me look after myself and you do the same."

I wiped the blood off my sword, slid it back into

its sheath, and took up my gun. "Got it?"

A mixture of emotions flickered across his face. Regret, anger, fear…

I felt a pang in my heart for causing him pain, but I would not have anyone sacrifice their safety for mine just because some unknown person demanded them to.

10

I woke to the thwump thwump of helicopter blades in the distance. Hoping our tent had arrived, I jumped to my feet and joined Fawke at the entrance to our soon-to-be abandoned home.

Two people exited the chopper, a third parachute following. I turned and grabbed my weapons. "Newcomers."

Fawke reached out to stop me. "I'll go with you. It's safer."

I nodded. I'd been so excited to see more humans to join our ranks, I'd forgotten the Malignants would lie in wait for them to hit the ground. The monsters knew the sound of an arriving chopper as well as I did. "Let's make it fast. If that's our tent, I want to leave soon. The rest of you load the wagons."

With Fawke leading the way, as usual, we stepped from our shelter and sprinted to the drop location. Shrieks rose around us. The monsters knew they were at risk of losing a good meal.

The newcomers, a man and a woman both dressed in leather, were deep in a battle when we arrived. The man slashed with a knife in one hand and shot a handgun with the other. The woman struggled, staying close to her companion's side.

Having been slowed down by the package dropped with them, they'd been surrounded. I started shooting on the run, switching to my sword when we were close enough for hand-to-hand combat. The Malignants might be many and strong, but they weren't fast or smart. The four of us were able to dispose of them easily enough.

"Crynn Dayholt. Leader." I held out my hand. "This is Fawke Newton."

The woman stared at the blood smeared across my skin and grimaced. "We're Orions. I'm Lara, this is Shane. I'll pass on the handshake for now."

I shrugged. "Follow us, quickly. More Malignants will come. You can tell us your stories once we're safe."

"Our stories?" Shane snorted. "We were starving, stole a loaf of bread, and here we are." He kicked a rock, sending it scuttering across the cracked concrete. With a heavy sigh, he grabbed one handle of the crate while Fawke took the other.

"More than a tent in here," Fawke said. "It's heavy."

"Early supplies?" I arched a brow.

"Possibly. Sharon does know we're about ready to leave on the President's stupid quest."

I nodded and led the way, keeping my eyes open for creatures skirting the shadows. I spotted a few, but no groups large enough to want to take on four armed humans.

Once we rejoined the others, I made the introductions and grabbed a crowbar to open the crate. "Yes!" A large water-resistant tent lay folded inside with cans of food and more water purification tablets. "We leave in the morning."

"For where?" Shane frowned. "We just got here."

"We've been assigned the task of heading to the mountains in search of other survivors." I left everything inside the crate. "It's going to be a long hard journey, so get your rest today."

"Survivors?" Lara glanced around the group. "Soriah is all there is."

"Nope." Kira shook her head. "That's what we all thought, too. We've seen the smoke in the distance."

I studied the two newcomers. Other than the leather suits they wore, they weren't heavily armed, and neither carried a backpack. "Were you not given access to the weapons room? Or allowed to fill packs?"

"We were chipped, then given a handgun and a knife and told to take the crate with us when we landed," Shane said, dropping to a cross-legged sitting position next to the fire. "Good thing there's food in there, huh? Lara and I won't go hungry anymore."

"How long did they send you for?" Dante asked, handing them each a tin cup of water.

"Life." The man's shoulders slumped. "Life in hell for a loaf of bread."

I glanced at Fawke. The astonished expression on his face told me he felt as surprised as I did at such a harsh punishment.

"Why'd you steal?" Ezra reclined on his blanket. "You had to know the consequences of breaking the law."

"We have two children." Tears spilled from Lara's eyes. "Shane wasn't making enough to keep them fed. Now, they're in the orphanage and we're here."

My heart dropped to my knees. These parents would never see their children again. The shining point was that the children wouldn't go hungry either. "I'm sorry. Rest today." I turned away and moved to the entrance.

Was this my fault? I'd asked for more fighters. Would Soriah send anyone who broke the law? I wanted help, but not at the expense of a family.

"What's wrong?" Fawke put a hand on my shoulder.

I hitched my chin. "I think this is how we'll get the fighters we need. Senseless, over-the-top, punishments."

"We do need them. Shane looked pretty capable out there today."

"Lara didn't. She isn't a fighter."

"She'll have to learn or Shane will lose her to."

We stared outside in silence for a few minutes, each lost in our thoughts. "How far have you ventured from this building?" I asked.

"Maybe a mile or two. After that, traveling is difficult. Too much debris. It's going to be hard with the wagons. We'll have to stop a lot to clear our way." He leaned against the wall.

"That might be why no one has ever seen any

scouts. They don't think it's worth the trouble." Which meant any other survivors might not know we exist.

He nodded. "There will be hordes of Malignants, too. We keep this area manageable. Unless someone has been clearing the area further on, then they've been allowed to thrive. They run in packs, so they will have found others and multiplied their numbers. Be glad of whatever help those on the hill send. Sad story or not, we need more people."

I stepped out and walked around the wagons. A small one for our supplies, the larger one for our tent. We'd be crowded like sardines. If our group grew, some would have to sleep under the trailer. They'd still be kept safe from rain.

Turning, I gazed across the cleared courtyard, evidence of years of hard work by Stalkers. Now, here I was, an eighteen-year-old, believing I could lead a ragtag team across this cement jungle full of monsters. I turned my attention to the mountain. No plume of smoke rose in the distance today. Perhaps the fire had been set by scouts skirting the edges of this once mighty metropolis.

How long until we ran into them? Would they be friendly or want to take what was ours?

"You aren't handling this alone," Fawke said. "We're all in this together."

"We could all die together." I glanced over my shoulder.

"Then we die. But," he gave a crooked grin, "we die fighting."

"Small consolation." I returned his smile, despite the fear churning in my gut. The fact I'd taken to a life of fighting so easily scared me. This place changed a person. Maybe not for the best.

"You're a good leader, Crynn. Don't doubt yourself. If you do, there are some here that will lose respect and not follow your lead."

Ezra. I took a deep breath, releasing it slowly. "Let's get some rest. I want to leave right after breakfast."

"What's the plan?" Moses glanced up from darning a sock. "This won't be a walk in the park."

"Who here has seen a park?" Gage asked. "How do you know? Before I came here, all I knew was concrete. Here…concrete and fires."

"There's trees on the mountain," Jolt added. "Probably spindly ones, but at least there's trees."

I mended a few of my own items of clothing as the others dreamed of how life on the mountain might be different from where we were. I didn't want to dwell on what ifs. Instinct told me the life here was going to feel like a piece of chocolate, smooth and sweet, over what awaited us out there.

"Have you seen the trees?" Gage arched a brow.

"No, but mountains have trees. I saw a picture in a book." Jolt gave a one shoulder shrug. "Don't dash my dreams, Miss Blue."

She laughed. "Only fools have dreams."

"I have a dream," Dante said softly. "When my time is up, I'm going to get married and have kids. I'll be living a life of luxury. Why not share it with someone? I've only got a year left."

"Must be nice," Kira muttered.

"I guess you shouldn't have killed someone." Dante's eyes narrowed.

"Some people don't deserve to live."

"Sexual assault," Moses whispered to me. "Attempted. Poor idiot didn't get a second chance."

"I would have killed him, too." I tied the string in a knot and bit off the end, tossing the pair of stockings back in my pack. I did a quick inventory of my few personal belongings, then zipped the bag closed and leaned back against it. All I owned could be worn or carried on my body at one time if needed. It was still more than I'd owned back home.

"What's your dream, Crynn?" Fawke smiled my way.

"To make it out of here alive."

"Hear, hear," the others cheered, raising mock glasses.

"That's the best dream." Fawke poked at the fire with a steel rod. Embers rose on a slight breeze smelling of death and decay.

"I used to tell my children scary stories of creatures that lived in the city," Lara said. "I thought it all just that. A story. Then I jumped off that plane. When I heard them, then saw them, I almost dropped dead. All my dreams have been shattered." She wrapped her arms around her bent knees. "I could care less if I live to see tomorrow."

Shane put his arm around her. "You still have me."

She leaned her head against him. "For now."

I knew I had to get her to want to live, to fight. I needed her to realize how valuable each and every one of us was, but she wouldn't hear me. She needed time to grieve. Tomorrow was a good enough time for me to set her straight. This life left no room for self-pity.

The next morning, Kira served us all a bowl of watery gray oats and weak tea. "It's not much, but it's hot. We've a long day ahead of us."

"Everything goes on the wagons." I dug into my meal. "We need our hands free and to be light on our feet. There's hard work and a lot of fighting to be done. Moses and Ezra will pull the sleeping trailer. It's big, but won't have anything on it but the tent. Shane and Lara will pull the supply trailer. The rest of us will stand guard, ready for attack. Questions?"

When none came, I finished eating and rinsed my bowl. The others followed suit, then tossed their packs on the trailer. Since Dante had dug up the hole we stored our supplies in the day before, all we had to do was load what little there was.

I took a deep breath and glanced around the place I'd called home for almost a month. Would we find water? Would Sharon keep her word at dropping our weekly supplies? Worry filled my mind like rocks pebbled the landscape.

My chin quivered. No tears! Alga's words rang out.

Squaring my shoulders, I gripped my gun and left the safety of the building. The others followed, taking up the positions I'd laid out for them.

A new chapter. One that would be harder than the last. I hadn't thought anything worse than being dropped outside Soriah. I knew life would show me just how wrong I'd been.

"Scarves up." I pulled mine over my face, hiding the fresh black stripes I'd put on that morning. "Eyes open, ears alert. Let's move people."

11

Night had fallen by the time we reached the first pile of debris. A building had toppled into the street, quickly being taken over by dirt and weeds.

Groans rose from the group as men released the handles on the wagons. Without being told, they grabbed whatever they could use to dig and hoist and got to work. Kira and I stood guard. Lara moved small stones, tossing them into a pile with the speed of a sloth.

"This is ridiculous." I shook my head. "Lara, switch jobs with Kira." I lowered my voice. "It's obvious she isn't strong and an even weaker fighter. Do you mind letting her take over the cooking?"

"Not at all." Kira grinned. "I'd rather have something more physical to do anyway."

I informed Lara of her new position. "You stand guard with me. If we have to fight, step back out of the way."

"I'm not completely worthless." Her face

darkened.

"Then prove it." I hated to be mean, but we had too much work to do and far too much danger around us for someone unable to carry their weight.

Shrieks reached us from the other side of the debris. Jolt scrambled up, nimber as a goat. "Holy Cow! There's way too many Malignants for us to clear."

My blood ran cold. "How do we move forward?"

Fawke joined Jolt at the top. "We can pick off a lot of them from up here. Shoot them down, maybe scare some of them off."

In my opinion, those things were too stupid to be scared off. "Everyone with a long range gun climb up. The rest of you guard down here." I reached up a hand for Fawke to pull me alongside him.

Jolt hadn't been kidding. A large horde of Malignants sprinted our way. It wouldn't take them long to scale the pile of debris.

"Fire!" I aimed and pulled the trigger.

When our weapons slowed, needing to power back up, we returned to the safer side of the fallen building. I slumped against the wall. A fifteen-minute breather would be nice. "Eyes open. There's time for some of them to make it over. Have your swords ready." My breathing came in pants.

Without more fighters we'd never complete this mission handed to us. I pushed away from the wall and turned on the radio. Let Sharon hear the shrieks behind us. Let her see if a Malignant came over the top.

The radio sat silent. After five minutes, I turned it off, hoping Sharon would call back.

Lara screamed.

I whirled in time to see three Malignants leap toward us. Gripping my sword, I joined the others. Taking care of three was an easy task, but more ventured over, their yellow eyes glittering as they spotted their prey.

I glanced at my gun. The light showing its power had turned to yellow instead of red. Only a few more minutes until it glowed green. We could hold them off that long.

"Sure wish we had a flame thrower," Jolt said. "I started to grab one, but I got ushered out of the supply room too fast."

"They have flame throwers?" I widened my eyes.

"Yep. Maybe you could request a couple?"

I could sure try. Anger boiled at having to ask for everything. Those on the hill in Soriah should send us what we needed without us having to ask. If they lost us to the Malignants, the next group of Stalkers would be fresh and untrained. If the wheel landed on a black square. If someone broke the law. Too many ifs for me.

As more came over, Jolt grabbed the nearest weapon and mowed them down. A big grin split his face.

"You're actually enjoying this." How is that possible?

"It sure beats working in the mines."

"The mines are safer."

"Are they?" He glanced over his shoulder. "Working ten hours a day in the pitch dark, hoping and praying to the Supreme Being that it doesn't cave in? Nah, I'll take this over that anytime."

"As much as I'm ready for my time here to be over," Fawke said, "I agree with Jolt. If I survive this place, I'll live in luxury on the hill. Those in the mines work there until they die."

"I'd prefer being a maid over this." I grabbed my gun. "Lara, mealtime, please. We'll eat in shifts, then resume clearing this pile." It would take us a few days. Until then, we'd also have to sleep in shifts.

After a quick bite of dried meat, washed down with tepid water, we resumed clearing, shooting, rinse and repeat. The task seemed hopeless.

Gage seemed to always be close to Fawke. I exhaled heavily, doing my best to ignore her loving gazes, and failing miserably. Of course, the two would be close. I was the newcomer here. Relationships would have been forged long before I arrived.

With ten of us, we paired up to take one-hour shifts, me and Dante being the first to guard while the others piled onto the larger wagon. With no threat of rain, I'd opted not to have the tent set up. If we were overrun, the others could fire without the impediment of canvas blocking their view.

"Is this the plan?" Dante asked, reclining against a pile of rocks. "To dig, shoot, sleep, and do the same the next day?"

"Unless you have a better idea." I remained standing, keeping my eyes focused on the pile we'd barely made a dent in. "If we could find a way around this, we could move faster."

"Send someone out in the morning to scout." He stuck a twig in his mouth, working it around with his tongue. "It might be easier to move rusty vehicles than this building."

"If there was an easier way, the Malignants would have found it and attacked."

"Maybe. I still think it's worth a try."

After an hour, Fawke and Gage took our place.

"All's quiet," I said, moving past them and onto the wagon.

"At least those things need sleep like we do," Fawke said. "Get some rest."

While I was grateful for having taken first watch and being able to get several hours of sleep in a row, I lay on my back, pillow flattening under me, and stared at the dark sky. This land had two versions of dark. Gray and black. What I wouldn't give to see the stars I'd read about.

My mother had always told me reading was a waste of time. Nothing in those pages existed anymore. I disagreed. Reading those words had filled me with hope that maybe the world could return to some semblance of that once-upon-a time.

Tears clogged my throat at how much I missed her. Did she think of me every day? The only consolation I had was the fact if I were to perish, she'd be notified. She wouldn't have to wait to see whether I returned at the end of my ten-year-assignment.

Shane and Lara murmured from the far end of the wagon, wrapped together as a married couple did, taking comfort in each other's arms. I sighed and rolled to my side, wishing for sleep to overtake me.

From the pile of concrete gave the soft conversation of Gage and Fawke. Loneliness assailed me, an emotion alien to me. Being an only child, I spent a lot of time alone. Here I lay, surrounded by others, and had never felt so alone.

"It gets easier," Kira whispered.

"What does?"

"This life."

"I've been here a month."

"It still will." She patted my shoulder. "Don't worry about Fawke. He doesn't care for Gage the same way she does him. I've seen the way he looks at you."

I rolled to face her. "Forming an attachment here would be foolish."

She laughed. "Yet, we're human, therefore we do foolish things."

"What about you?"

"I'm a lifer. If I want…companionship, I hook up with Ezra. Goodnight, Crynn."

I didn't want companionship. I wanted a life with a husband and children. All I had to do was make it to my twenty-eight birthday. Yeah, good luck with that.

I woke the next morning to the smell of brewing coffee. I bolted up. Coffee?

Lara smiled and handed me a cup. "I managed to filch some from the supply room. We were only given fifteen minutes. I kept it hidden until I thought we could really use a cup."

"Awesome, but don't do that again. We can't have secrets among us." I sipped, wishing for sugar, but almost giddy to have it black. I glanced around the others who seemed as pleased as I did. "Did you manage anything else?"

She cut a quick glance at her husband. "Thread,

needles, a few medical supplies." She started pulling things from her pockets. "I've been a thief my whole life. It's how my family survived when I was a child. Shane hates it."

"But he was arrested for stealing."

She shook her head. "I stole the bread. He went along with me so they wouldn't send me away with him. I know that sounds horrible, since we have children, but our children are now being fed on a regular basis. Sleeping in real beds. Receiving an education. It's better that we both had to leave rather than one."

"You'll never see them again."

She drew a shuddering breath. "My hope is that someone will adopt them and give them a better life than they could ever have had with me."

I couldn't imagine making that kind of choice. My childhood had been hard. Especially after my father died, but my mother would never have chosen a life of crime or given me up. "Thanks for the coffee." I got to my feet and joined the others who stared at the mound of concrete and rocks.

"Dante told me of his idea." Fawke glanced my way. "He also told me of your response."

"Do you think I'm wrong?" I arched a brow.

"Not entirely. I think it warrants investigating. We might not find a place big enough for the wagons, but maybe we'll find an area requiring less work to clear. Feel up to a walk?"

"Sure. We'll leave after breakfast. What about the others?"

"They can stay here and keep working in case we don't find anything." He took a sip from his cup.

"Did you reprimand her for hiding this from us?"

"In a way. She had other things, too. Helpful items."

"Do you think she's still hiding things?"

I shrugged. "I've bigger things to worry about. She's here for life anyway. What bigger punishment could I dish out?"

"True."

After another meal of watered down gruel, I collected my weapons, left Ezra in charge, much to his surprise, and set out with Fawke. "We need to find a water source. We can't let our supply run out."

"I agree. Rationing will come. It's best if we push that off as far as possible."

We fell in step together, following the line of the fallen building. I cast several apprehensive glances around as we moved farther from the group. The two of us would be no match for a horde the size of the one that waited for us on the other side of the blockage. The others wouldn't be either.

Fawke and I could not be gone long. Once the Malignants were on the move again, attack on the group was imminent. I actually wished for rain to keep the creatures inside.

12

Senses alert, Fawke and I searched without speaking. The air filled with the sound of shrieks and the nauseating odor of decay.

Occasionally, Fawke would hold up his fist to call a halt, listen, then wave me forward. The pile of rubble on our left started to taper until I could peer over the edge without standing on my tip-toes. Good news in that it showed we might find an easier path, bad news in that if we could see over so could the Malignants.

We picked up our pace, coming to a break in the debris blocked by a couple of rusted out vehicles. If we could push those aside, we could pull the wagons through. Spotting a group of monsters too large for the two of us to fight ourselves, we turned around and headed at a sprint to the others.

"Thought we were going to have to call in the army," Ezra said. "You were gone half the day."

"We are the army." I flashed a grin. "We also

found an easier way."

"Good thing. We aren't making much progress here, and those things are too close for comfort." He called for everyone to pack up.

I shrugged. I'd left him in charge. Obviously, it wasn't a cloak he could easily shuck. I accepted a piece of dried meat and a small bit of water from Lara and sat to rest while the others loaded up.

"See anyone?" Moses sat next to me.

"Just Malignants." I cut him a sideways glance. "You think we'll run into people so soon?"

He nodded. "Follow me to the top."

Exhaling heavily, I rushed my lunch and climbed to the top of the debris pile. I scanned the horizon, not seeing anything but Malignants emerging from buildings until Moses pointed.

"The weeds are trampled across that courtyard."

"So?" The path through more vehicles and fallen buildings could have been made by the creatures.

"I've never known these things to make a path. They clamber over. Why bother? Plus…" He handed me a pair of binoculars. "What do you see?"

I lifted the piece to my eyes and took a longer look. A green backpack and a sword lay in the path. A few feet on I spotted the remains of who they'd once belonged to. "Not one of our former members?"

"Nope. We've not gone this far before."

I climbed down and turned on the radio. "Come on, answer."

"What is it?" Sharon's face filled the screen.

"We need more people."

"There aren't any."

I put on my sternest expression. "Take some from

the prison. We've wasted two days trying to clear a path. On the other side of this pile is a horde of Malignants. If we die, you won't have your answers."

Her eyes widened. "You want me to send murderers?"

"Why not? Give them the option of fighting with us or staying behind bars." I felt pretty certain they'd choose to fight with us.

Fawke narrowed his eyes, clearly not in agreement with me. Maybe I should have consulted the group, but where else would we get the able bodies we need?

"We need help clearing our way and fighting. We're grossly out-numbered." I refused to back down.

"That would mean more supplies, Miss Dayholt."

"The prisoners are being fed now, aren't they?" I tilted my head. "It's a matter of sending their food here. I'm sure that's something you can handle."

Bright spots of color appeared on her pale cheeks. "You're very close to overstepping your bounds."

I leaned closer to the monitor. "I'm responsible for these people. I take that seriously. Send us help or we don't go any further."

After a tense few minutes of staring at each other, she nodded. "I'll get back to you before you retire for the night."

When her image disappeared, I turned to the others. "We'll keep moving toward the spot Fawke and I found. Hopefully, we'll hear from her before nightfall."

"That's pretty gutsy, boss." Ezra shook his head, grinning. "What if she used your chip to dispose of you?"

"I'm not sure the chip can do that." I hefted my pack onto the wagon. "I think it's simply there to track us. Moses showed me evidence of another human on the other side of this expanse of concrete. We aren't alone out here."

Shock rippled across the faces of my comrades. "But prisoners?" Kira shook her head. "I mean…half of us are criminals, only the hardened ones are sent to prison."

"You'd think they'd be the most expendable, don't you?" I shrugged.

"Can you handle murderers, Crynn?" Fawke asked. "The men she sends might not take orders from a tiny slip of a girl."

"If they don't, we'll send them on alone. They'll never survive without us." I put my hands on my hips and glanced from one face to the other. "Do you want to do this without more fighters?"

"No." A muscle ticked in his jaw. "We need the help."

"What if they try to molest us?" Gage's voice rose. "They probably haven't seen a woman in who knows how long."

"Sleep with your knife in one hand." I saw her point, but wasn't going to back down. I didn't know of any other way to get help. The Wheel was too slow. We didn't have that kind of time. "Let's move."

"You heard her." Fawke fell into step beside me.

"I'll do what I can to make sure your authority is recognized."

"Thank you." I'd taken a gutsy move, one I prayed would work.

"What makes you think the chip is merely a tracker?"

"Have you ever heard of one being detonated?"

"No."

I grinned. "Ezra has been here for a long time. Don't you think he'd have shared such a tale over a nighttime fire?"

He laughed, clapping me on the shoulder. "You've quite the brain inside that pretty head."

My face flushed at his compliment. "I've read a lot of books."

"Thank the Supreme Being for that." He stepped back to help pull the wagons.

Kira took his place. "I feel exposed." She jerked her head to where the toppled building tapered.

"We'll have to fight." Why weren't the Malignants climbing over to get to us? "Stay ready. We could be walking into a trap." If those things weren't coming over, they'd be coming through, making it easier for us to pick them off.

The wagons clattered over rocks and iron beams making our presence known. Still no creatures attacked. I peered over the building. Where were they?

"Something has drawn them away," Kira said. "What would do that?" She glanced at the sky. "Doesn't look like rain."

I held up my fist to call a halt a few feet away from flames over a crack in the asphalt. "Fawke, we need to scout ahead."

"I'll go," Jolt offered, releasing the handle of the wagon. It dropped with a thud. "Fawke is needed here more than I am. He's a better fighter."

"Which is why I go with Crynn." Fawke grabbed his gun.

Having him with me was more preferable than the less experienced Jolt. Plus, I enjoyed his company out from under the hungry gaze of Gage. "Fawke goes. The rest of you rest. We camp here tonight and head through the opening tomorrow. If Sharon calls, tell her I'll be back in an hour."

"She isn't going to like you taking command." Fawke grinned. "But, I like the bossy Crynn."

Unfortunately, he wasn't in control of my fate. What's the worst Soriah could do to me? Make me stay here for the rest of my life? A horrible fate, but one I could deal with if it kept my people safe. My family, as they'd become to me. This group was all I had.

We took off at a jog, slowing as we stepped through the opening we'd located earlier that day. I tensed, expecting an attack. Nothing. No shrieks, no sight of a single monster.

"Where are they?" I glanced at Fawke.

"I don't know, but I don't like it. This is eerie."

We stepped onto what might have once been a busy city street. Cars lined the sides, smashed as pieces of skyscrapers fell. A few fires burned where the asphalt had cracked.

Craning my neck, I stared at a building that still towered above the others. A light flickered in one of the windows. I tapped Fawke on the shoulder and pointed. Malignants didn't need light. We'd located another human.

"Do you think they're following whoever that is?" I asked.

"All of them?" Fawke frowned. "Whoever it is would be dead by now if that horde knew about their existence."

"Should we go in?"

"Yes, but stay behind me. If something happens, run back to the others."

"Not without you." I glared.

He exhaled sharply. "You know the special assignments?"

"Yeah."

"Well, mine is to keep our leader safe at all costs. I failed once, I won't fail again." He stepped into the darkness of the building.

That explained a lot. I still wouldn't let him, or anyone, jeopardize their life for me, though. Special assignment be damned. Praying the building wouldn't fall, I followed.

The odor inside was almost unbearable, making me glad for the scarf around my face. It didn't take the stench away, but did mask it some.

Fawke clicked on a flashlight, put a finger to his lips, and headed deeper into the building. A set of steel stairs led to the second floor. Something scraped above us. We froze.

When no more sound came, we continued upward. I gripped the rickety railing so tight my knuckles ached. Another scrape. Sweat poured down my brow. I preferred seeing the threat toward me rather than seeking it out.

The second floor held no walls. Fawke's light barely broke the darkness of the cavernous space. Yet it was here we'd seen the light, heard the sound of a foot scraping against cement. Fawke clicked off his light.

After a few seconds, my eyesight adjusted to the dark. I glanced around the room, venturing further in.

Piles of weeds and dried grass dotted the floor. We'd found a lair.

Fawke squatted next to one, turning his light back on. "Crynn." He pointed to grass matted with blood.

"Is that an umbilical cord?" I swallowed against the mountain in my throat.

"Yep. They're breeding."

"I didn't think they could."

"I'm finding out there's a lot we didn't know." He whirled and shined his light in a corner.

A young man held up his hands. "Don't shoot."

"Who are you?" I took a step closer, only to be stopped by Fawke.

"Nobody." The man whirled and dashed away, his steps echoing as he descended another staircase.

Fawke and I gave chase. We'd made our first contact with a human outside our group. I had no intention of letting him get away.

Outside, we chased him across the street and into another building. The back wall of the building had long ago been blasted away. Our prey darted through and across a small courtyard before scaling a fence.

We lost him in the next building. No sight or sound of him.

I kicked a rock, sending it clattering away from me. A shout rang out from a few yards away. I shot

Fawke a look when another voice rang out, then several and the sounds of a battle, sword against sword.

We'd located a group. Perhaps the very group of survivors we'd been sent to find.

Unfortunately, the horde of Malignants had found them as well.

13

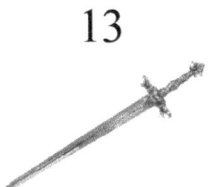

"This isn't our fight." Fawke's face tightened. "Two more fighters won't make a difference."

"You want to leave them to die?" I stared at two small groups of men fighting for their lives against way too many Malignants.

"They aren't your responsibility." He faced me. "The people waiting for us are."

My gut wrenched. He was right. As much as I hated to leave them, my obligation lay elsewhere. At least we now knew we weren't alone in this vast concrete jungle. I turned away, blinking back tears. "Let's go back. We know why those things aren't bothering us. That's what we came for."

"Crynn."

I turned around at the sternness in his voice. Two men, chased by three Malignants, sprinted our way. These two we could help. I whipped my gun from my shoulder and took aim.

Fawke did the same.

One of the men dropped to one knee and plunged his sword into the beast's belly.

I waved them on as other creatures took notice. With the distraction, other humans broke away from their group and headed into a dark building. Shrieks rang out as the monsters realized they'd lost their prey.

"Take down as many as you can," I ordered, mowing down the approaching beasts with my gun as Fawke followed suit. "You other two be ready in case any get past us."

They slumped against the fallen building, leaving the fighting to me and Fawke. After ridding the world of ten more Malignants, the creatures realized they fought a losing battle and darted away.

"You two come with us." I aimed my weapon on them, eyeing the packs the two wore. "We've a small group waiting for us."

"Who are you?" Fawke stepped forward, glaring down at them.

Of course, we should ask that question first. Again, I wondered about the wisdom behind my appointment as leader.

"Who are you?" A belligerent look crossed one of their faces.

"The ones who saved you," I said. "Hand over your packs and answer the question."

"Don't do it," Lars." The other one shook his head.

"We have one name." Fawke kicked the foot of the one who hadn't answered.

"Dayton." He tossed his pack, slamming me in the chest, then bolted to his feet.

"Stupid move since we have the guns." Fawke aimed at his chest. "Play nice or you'll regret not falling with your comrades."

"They weren't part of our group." Dayton crossed his arms. "We ran into them and a fight started. They wanted our packs, too. Then, those things showed up, and we had to fight together."

I opened the pack he'd thrown, my eyes widening at the sight of fabric, an ornate gold goblet, a sparkling necklace, and other luxuries I'd only read about. Nothing to help a person survive in the city wasteland. "What is this?"

"We work for Soriah," Lars said. "Oh, shut up, Dayton. We're blown. Might as well come clean. Besides, I'm sick and tired of risking my life for those rich people on the hill."

"You scavenge for Soriah?" Fawke's brow furrowed.

"Where else do you think they get their fancy items? When the city fell, things were left behind. It's up to us to find them and take them back."

"How?" I zipped up the pack.

"We leave them on top of a designated building. They get picked up." Dayton shrugged. "It isn't our place to ask questions."

"How many of you are there?"

"Well, there was five. I guess there's just the two of us now. The Wheel decides. Mind telling us who you are?"

"Stalkers," I answered. "The wheel landed on black. We're here to rid the city of those things." To make the job for scavengers easier was my guess.

"Did you see the box on the wheel with the

goblet? That's what determines our job. A chopper drops us off on the other side of the city. We've come a long way since then. Those things kept driving us farther and farther from the pickup site."

"Who were those you were fighting?"

"No idea. We didn't have time to ask questions."

I glanced at Fawke. How many different groups were out here? Our job just got harder. We had more than Malignants to deal with. "Let's go. It's getting dark." Maybe I could use the items these two found to bargain with Sharon for more people.

"There's food in this pack," Fawke said. "At least we won't have to share what little we have." He tossed the pack back. "This is Crynn Dayholt, our leader. I'm Fawke."

"She doesn't look old enough to lead an elementary class." Lars shook his head, getting to his feet.

"Looks can be deceiving." I prodded him forward with the barrel of my weapon.

As we made the long trek back to the others, I thought on how I'd handle Sharon when she called again. I couldn't keep it secret that we had these two, not if I wanted to bargain with the luxury items. She'd most likely tell me these two were now a part of us. They weren't enough. We needed more fighters. What I didn't know was whether I'd tell her about the other group. I didn't want to give her too much information until I had answers to some of my questions. The main one being…what the heck were we really doing out there?

The others glanced up from where they rested around the fire as we approached. Ezra got to his feet.

"Sharon didn't mention dropping anyone off when she called."

"I missed her?" I tossed one of the packs on the wagon.

"She'll call back."

"We saved these two from Malignants," I said. "Lars and Dayton. Scavengers for Soriah. There was another group, but they ran off when we distracted those things." I sat on a cement block, grateful to be off my feet.

"The ones we're looking for?" Ezra glanced in the direction we'd come.

"No idea who they are." I shot him a warning look. We didn't need to reveal too much to the newcomers. Not until we knew whether we could trust them.

He took the hint. "Want me to tie them up?"

"After we eat." I doubted they'd run at the promise of a meal. "Check the other pack. It's got supplies."

"Those are ours." Dayton glared.

"We share everything. Since you're here, this belongs to all of us." I lay my weapon across my knees.

Lara handed me a bowl of the same gruel we'd ate for breakfast. "I know it isn't much."

"It's fine. There isn't much variety out here." The food was filling and gave us strength. That's all that mattered. "Fawke and I will take first watch. We've had a long day and can use several hours of uninterrupted sleep. These two can be tied under the wagon. It looks like rain. Everyone else sleep in your rubber suits." I dug into my bowl, more ravenous than I'd thought.

As I spooned the last bite into my mouth, Sharon's face filled the radio monitor. I got up and stood in front of it. "I hope you have good news for me."

"It appears you have two more."

"Right. The trackers." I smiled without humor. "Nothing gets past you."

"We want what they found."

"And I want more fighters. Care to make an exchange?"

"You may keep the two you found."

"They aren't enough." I crossed my arms. "We need extra provisions, suits, weapons, and living humans. The rest of their group were overrun with Malignants. The deeper we go into the city, the more of those things we encounter. Unless you want us all to suffer the same fate as the other scavengers, you'll send help."

"Our conversations have grown very redundant, Miss Dayholt. President Cane is not pleased at your lack of servility."

"That's unfortunate." I kept my smile in place. "Perhaps we could trade places."

Her features hardened. "Your insolence is unbecoming to your position. Five minor criminals will arrive tomorrow. Get the luxury items to the top of the nearest tall building. The items for fighters." The screen went black.

Dayton clapped. "Bravo. You might be young, but you're either the bravest or stupidest person I've ever met."

"A little bit of both," Ezra said. "Welcome to the

crazy farm." He pulled some plastic rope from our supplies and tied the newcomers together under the wagon. "Sleep tight. How long you here for?"

"Twenty years, but every item of value we find takes off a year. I have fifteen left. Lars is down to eighteen."

"I'm a lifer, so don't try to escape. Killing you won't extend my sentence." Ezra marched back to his spot next to the fire.

Dayton cursed and wiggled against his bindings until Lars yelled for him to stop.

I chuckled and climbed to the top of the debris pile to start my hour's watch. A few minutes later, Fawke joined me.

"Now, we're twelve."

"Maybe." I peered through the dark for any signs of life, beast or human. "Do you think we can trust them?"

"They heard Sharon's orders. They have no choice but to be a part of our group."

"You still think we can be killed by our chip."

"I'm not willing to find out. Not this close to the end of my term."

I'd miss him when he left. If I lived another two years.

"Five more isn't enough." I sighed.

"Don't press your luck. Seventeen is a lot more than I thought we'd ever get. Pray some more young unfortunates land on black on their eighteenth birthday."

What a horrible thing to wish, yet I did. Very much. I hated this place, the system, Sharon, President Cane…the list seemed endless. Dwelling on what I disliked would do me, or the others, no good. I had to make the best of things. "I'd rather pray that we receive enough supplies for the group."

"That's a good prayer, too." He bumped me with his shoulder. "Chin up. I've survived this long, you will, too."

"Before now, the group stayed in their safe little courtyard, dispelling Malignants as they came close."

"Awaiting orders. Your arrival changed it all."

I narrowed my eyes through the gloom. "No, that plume of smoke in the distance changed it all. My arrival happened at the right time, unfortunately."

"Things have definitely gotten more exciting."

I laughed despite my bad mood. "You are a strange person, Fawke Newton."

"Trying to see the bright side of things."

How could anything be bright in a world of different shades of gray? I shook my head and focused my attention back on the expanse in front of us. Far off, I thought I saw a light flicker. Wishful thinking or exhaustion?

If we could find the group that had run into the buildings, maybe we could convince them to join us. Either that or fight. I didn't want to pull my weapon against another human. There weren't enough of us anymore.

"Any idea how to make Lars and Dayton cooperate?"

"I know you don't believe the chip can kill, but I'm sure they do. Threaten them with that."

He was right. I did believe the chip to be nothing more than a tracker. I didn't want to test it, though, and I came very close each time I butted heads with Sharon. If I could be exterminated that way, I must have value since I still breathed.

The far-off light flickered again, this time farther away. Whoever patrolled the night headed away from us and therefore posed no threat. Another scavenger or someone else?

Moses and Kira took next watch. I climbed into the tent, fluffed my pillow, and refused to think further on the things I hated. Instead, I focused on what I did have. A new family, the skill of fighting, and the ability to get Sharon to do what I wanted.

I smiled. It would be enough. For a while, anyway.

The presence of close bodies kept me warm, and I drifted off to sleep dreaming of the life I'd have in ten years. One where I never worried about food or shelter or fighting creatures thirsty for blood.

14

Over another bowl of gruel the next morning I pondered who to take to the nearest tall building and who to leave behind to guard the supplies. With scavengers and the mystery group roaming the city, our supplies would be very enticing. I could leave ten behind and pray Fawke and I could safely meet up with the arriving five and stay alive in the process.

I could send Ezra with him, but as leader, I felt it my duty to take on the more dangerous tasks. Why have someone do something I wasn't willing to? If I perished, the next poor fool to land on black would be sent to take my place same as any of them.

Pushing to my feet, I told the others to stay behind and pull the wagons out of sight. "Fawke will go with me." I eyed Lars and Dayton. "If you two cause any trouble, I'll have your chips detonated. Run and I'll shoot you the moment I see you. You heard Sharon. You're with us now. Prove we can trust you."

"I'm in no hurry to die," Dayton said. "You'll have no trouble from me." He handed me the pack with the luxury items. "Lars and I aren't stupid. Good luck getting the same attitude from those you're meeting up with."

I nodded, hoping the released prisoners would cooperate because they were no longer behind bars. Not cooperating could easily result in their death. If they ran, they'd die for sure. I doubted any of them would be seasoned fighters. I slung the pack over my shoulder and motioned my head for Fawke to lead the way.

"During our watch last night," he took the pack from me and put it on himself, "I spotted a tall building that looked as if it might support the weight of several people."

"Not the chopper?"

"I don't think they'll land. The pilot will most likely hover and let the others jump off." He inhaled long and deep. "With all these newbies, we're going to have to take a day or two to teach them fighting skills. It'll be too dangerous to have to babysit so many inexperienced people."

"We can hold up for a while. If Sharon complains, we'll explain why."

He laughed. "You mean you'll tell her and leave no room for argument."

I grinned. "Yep."

"Let's hope your luck with her continues. I don't think Soriah has ever met anyone as strong willed as you."

His words sounded like a compliment and filled

me with a rush of warmth. "This may be none of my business, but are you and Gage an item?" The words spewed out before I could stop them.

He stopped and faced me. "With only two years left on my time, why would I get involved with anyone here? Especially someone with nine years left."

Which meant I had no chance. I shrugged. "That makes sense."

"Why'd you ask?" His eyes twinkled.

"Seems like folks pair up on occasion. It's a lonely life out here."

"I don't mind being alone." He resumed our hike.

I stifled a sigh and matched my pace to his. We'd set off early enough that I hoped we wouldn't run into too many Malignants. At least not until we retrieved the newcomers to our group. I also hoped they came with weapons, guns preferably. Every member of our group needed a long-range rifle and a sword.

A rock clattered to my right. I whirled in time to see a large rat scurry out of sight. The question as to what the Malignants ate when they couldn't kill a human was answered. Rats would be easy prey to feed their offspring.

"If we ever find a nest," I said, "we have to dispose of it."

Fawke arched a brow. "Of course."

Stupid statement. My face flushed. "Killing young will be easier than the adults."

Again, his expression said I stated the obvious. "You know what I mean. We're here to find survivors, but that doesn't release us from ridding the city of Malignants."

"Again, that's obvious. By us clearing the way, scavengers have an easier time filling the coffers of the rich." Bitterness dripped from his words.

My steps faltered. Fawke rarely showed displeasure with the life he'd been dealt. Did things get mentally harder the closer a person got to their date of freedom? Of course, we'd discovered a lot of deceit in the last few days. Lies told by Soriah to get us to do their bidding.

Fawke slipped through the same opening we'd discovered the day before and halted. "Coast is clear. See that building across the way? It's got to be ten stories tall. It should suffice for the chopper."

"If it isn't full of Malignants."

"Move as quietly as possible. Our suits will hide our scent."

True. But I doubted those we were meeting would be dressed in the same suits. I glanced at the sky, relieved not to see any rain clouds. If Sharon really listened to my requests, the newcomers would arrive with a crate containing what they needed to survive out here. We weren't as expendable as Soriah once thought.

We sprinted down the street toward the building Fawke had chosen. Inside, we stopped and pulled the scarves from our nose and mouth. The air reeked, warning us of Malignants inside.

I pulled my scarf back up to hide the black stripes and make breathing a little easier, then followed Fawke toward a set of stairs. Ten flights. Ugh.

We saw little sign of the creatures in the cement-walled stairwell. A few fresh smears on the wall that looked like blood. They'd brought their kills from yesterday here.

"Keep your eyes open for weapons," Fawke whispered. "Anything else we can use. If they brought the dead here, they could have been wearing packs."

That would be an easy score. I remembered the pack I'd spotted across the way a couple of days ago. We'd need to see if it was still there if others hadn't found it first. We weren't in any position to let anything useable lie out to rot.

On the fourth floor we found the remains of the first body in the middle of a nest. No sign of the nest's occupants, but I heard shrieks from a distance away. The Malignants had left their lair to hunt.

We searched the room for anything useable, finding a knife and a small bottle of water purification tablets. I confiscated them and continued following Fawke to the next floor. Score. A backpack lay next to the remains of another body.

I opened it to reveal vegetable seeds and articles of clothing. I grinned. Sharon didn't know of these things. I could use them to barter with. In a city of overcast skies, no vegetables would grow. Only Soriah had the means to make artificial sunlight.

By the time we reached the roof, we hadn't found anything else, and my lungs burned from the climb. I slid to the cold concrete roof to rest until the chopper arrived. I pulled a canteen from my belt, took a deep drink, then handed it to Fawke who sat next to me.

"Thanks." He didn't look as if he'd just climbed ten flights of stairs. He wasn't panting for breath or wiping sweat from his brow. How did he continue on as if everything was an afternoon stroll?

I leaned my head back and closed my eyes. We were safe enough on the roof. With only one door leading to us, we'd pick off any Malignants who dared follow. "I hope we don't have long to wait. I want to search the area the fighting occurred yesterday."

"Me, too. I'd like to get back before dark." He took another drink from the canteen and handed it back to me. "It'll be slow going if a crate arrives with the five new people and we run into Malignants."

We always ran into them. The creatures were an infestation. I couldn't remember how long ago the world had gone dark or when the plague released. Way before my time. Even before my parents. I'd once heard it had happened a hundred years ago. I didn't think anyone thought it possible the Malignants would breed. I'm sure they believed they could eventually be killed off.

The thwump of an arriving chopper pulled me to my feet. I squared my shoulders and waited to see who Sharon had sent us.

The chopper hovered just off the rooftop. A crate was pushed off first, followed by two women and three men all forty-years-old and younger. At least we hadn't been sent any elderly people. These all looked strong enough to be of some worth. The two men dragged the crate toward us, then the five lined up as if for an inspection.

"I'm Crynn Dayholt, your leader. This is Fawke our top fighter."

The oldest man, his gray hair shaved close to his

head nodded and pointed to each person down the line. "Riva, Samson, Jep, Lotus, Zed. Thank you for asking for our release."

"Your crimes?"

He sneered. "I'm the only murderer here. Killed someone in a drunken brawl. You won't have to worry about any of us. The air might be foul here, but at least we're in the open."

"Time will determine how grateful you are." I smiled. "Did they tell you what you'd be doing?"

"Spending the rest of our lives fighting monsters."

"Can you fight?"

"Time will tell." He chuckled.

"Let's see what we've been sent." I motioned for them to open the crate.

Seven rubber suits, two flame throwers, swords, food, and long-range rifles. My smile widened. Sharon really wanted us to live long enough to find the survivors Soriah sought.

"Don the rubber suits. It helps hide your scent. Then, each of you grab a gun and a sword. You'll need them before we get back to camp. Very little time passes without a battle."

The pretty woman named Lotus paled. "I'm here because I refused to accept my fate on the wheel. It landed on red. I'm not a fighter."

"You will be," Fawke said. "If you make it back to camp alive, I'll train you. If you don't learn, you'll die. That goes for all of you."

"How many of us are there?" The young man named Jep asked.

"You five make us seventeen."

"That's all." His eyes widened.

"That's it."

I waited for one of them to comment on my age, glad when they didn't. These people had been trained not to ask a lot of questions. Good. They'd follow orders without too much trouble.

Once they had donned the suits and picked up the crate, we headed down the stairs and onto the street. Lotus gasped as shrieks rose from an adjoining building.

"No sound," I hissed. "No sudden moves. The suits confuse them, but if you run or make too much noise, they'll attack."

Tears welled in her eyes. She nodded.

"And absolutely no tears. There's no room for weakness out here. If you must cry, do it in the privacy of your bed."

"You'll make a good replacement for Alga someday," Fawke said, his gaze warm on mine.

Pleased way more than I should be, I headed in the direction of the fight yesterday. Unless those who'd fled had returned, we'd find things they'd left behind. I didn't mind scavenging for the sake of my group. Why let Soriah's bloodhounds find everything?

15

"Let's show these newbies how it's done." Fawke held out his hand.

I slipped mine in his and got to my feet. We'd chosen the courtyard of a small building with a collapsed roof as our temporary camp. Surrounded by a block fence, we were protected by any surprise attacks. It was the perfect place to spar and train the others. Only one way in and that was by squeezing past an iron gate hanging by one hinge.

I pulled my sword and took up my stance, a grin spreading across my face. "I'm better than I used to be. Are you sure you don't want to use sticks?"

"That's good, and no. This way you'll fight harder to avoid my blade." He winked and attacked, his weight on his right leg.

This was no fancy dancing back and forth. This was a straight out brawl.

I swung my sword over my head, metal clanging as he blocked my sword. I spun and dropped to one knee, jabbing upward only to have him swing and block again.

The gazes of everyone in our group burned holes through me, fueling me to fight harder, fight faster. Sweat ran down my face, blurring my vision.

The flat side of Fawke's blade slapped against my backside eliciting screams and jeers from the others. "I don't think a Malignant is interested in that part of my body." I lunged. "They prefer guts." I knocked his sword aside, stopping my tip from mere inches from his belly.

"Bravo." He stopped and clapped. "Anger spurs you on."

"That and the will to live." I leaned against the fence to catch my breath. "The rest of you grab a thick stick. I'll work with the women?"

"Sounds good. Ezra and Moses are strong enough fighters to help with the men."

I sheathed my sword and found a stick as thick as my wrist. We didn't want any injuries worse than a bruise, and the sooner we deemed the new people fight worthy, the sooner we could resume our mission.

I paired Gage with Lara, Kira with Riva, and Lotus with Lara. I closely monitored the last two, them both being new to the group, and occasionally changed places with one or the other.

"Block your body at all times. When the attack comes, the monsters won't pussy-foot around. They come at you in full force. If you don't kill them, they will kill you. Don't be timid." I tapped my stick on Lara's shoulder. "Pretend you're protecting your babies."

That helped a little, but the woman was definitely not a fighter. I doubted she'd last a month out here.

After an hour, I called a fifteen-minute break, then resumed. "I'll spar with Kira. The rest of you watch and learn."

Kira wasn't as good as Fawke, but she gave me an intense workout. It might be a good idea to have regular sparring sessions to keep us all in top fighting shape. "Look." She pointed her stick to the sky.

A white parachute floated down toward the parking lot on the other side of the fallen building we'd camped next to yesterday. "Whoever that is won't survive the horde living there. Let's go, people." I pulled up my scarf and took off at a dead run.

Fawke passed me quickly. Pounding footsteps behind me let me know the others followed. We were going to be too late no matter how fast we ran.

"Over the top! There's no time to reach the opening." I scrambled up, my feet slipping on loose bricks and cement.

Up and over like ants, then a full sprint to where the person fought to free themselves of their chute. From the nearby buildings swarmed Malignants. Seconds later, screams came from under the chute which was now being ripped to shreds along with the person trapped underneath.

I held up my hand to stop the others. "We're too late. The horde is too big for us." My shoulders slumped. "We'll wait until nightfall to see what we can retrieve." Happy Birthday whoever you are.

Back at camp, I paced in front of my group. "That's what happens when you're unprepared. She should never have gotten tangled."

"She?" Dante tilted his head.

"Sounded like a female." I kicked a rock. The poor girl probably wouldn't have made it to us anyway. Not with the numbers of Malignants that swarmed her. We could have lost more by trying to save her.

"How are we supposed to get across that lot with that many of those things?" Lotus turned and lost her breakfast.

Fawke glanced my way. "Should we start traveling at night? The rubber suits have flashlights. It'll be slower, but they sleep at night."

I stopped my pacing. "I don't see that we have any other choice. Get some sleep people. We move out as soon as it's quiet." I sat with my back against the wall and closed my eyes. I didn't need to see to know Fawke sat next to me.

"It's unfortunate, but it happens. More than we'd like."

"How many since you've been here?"

"She made five. All the same way. They couldn't get out from under their chute in time." His voice held all the weariness I felt.

The radio crackled. My eyes snapped open as Sharon's face appeared on the monitor. "It's your job, Miss Dayholt, to make sure new arrivals don't die the moment they step foot on land."

"There was nothing I could do. The Malignants were too many for us to tackle." I would not let her make me feel any worse than I already did.

"We have more turning eighteen in a few days. Make sure if one arrives that you keep them alive."

The screen went black.

"How did she know?" Lotus asked.

"The chip we all have goes dead when our heart stops beating," Fawke said.

"We'll lose some of us as time goes by." Ezra sat next to one of the gas fires. "There's no way we can reach that mountain without a few deaths."

"Thank you, Mr. Encouragement." I glared.

"I don't want to go." Lara shook her head. "Leave me here. I'll die here. It's better than being torn apart."

"No one stays behind," I said.

"Let them activate my chip." She stared wide-eyed around the group, shrugging off her husband's hand as he tried to placate her. "What do I need to do?" She grabbed her stick. "Kill?" She whacked Lotus on the head. The girl crumbled to the ground.

I tackled Lara, yanking the stick from her hand. If her chip wasn't activated once Sharon found out, it would confirm my suspicions that they were nothing more than trackers.

Kira knelt next to Lotus. "She's alive, but she'll have one hell of a headache."

I stood and pulled Lara to her foot, then shoved her in the direction of her husband. "Take care of her or I'll use her as a distraction when we cross that lot. If she tries something that stupid again, I'll kill her myself."

Nodding, he led his wife to the other side of the courtyard, doing his best to calm her hysterics. "Shh. It'll be okay."

Idiot. I moved over and patted Lotus's cheek. "Open your eyes."

They fluttered open. "Why'd she hit me?"

"A failed attempt at suicide, I think." Seeing that the woman would be fine, I pressed the button on the radio to call Sharon.

"So soon, Miss Dayholt?"

I explained what had happened. "She's a nuisance to us."

"Have you handled the situation? As leader, it's up to you to reprimand."

"The chip?" I arched a brow.

"You know as well as I do that isn't possible." The screen went black.

"All these years it was nothing but a lie?" Ezra's face darkened. "A ploy to manipulate us?"

"I'm surprised no one thought to test it before now." I resumed my seat against the wall and watched as Kira gave Lotus an extra ration of water.

"What made you suspect?" Dante asked.

"I read everything I can get my hands on. It didn't make sense that they'd kill off someone who most likely wouldn't make it to their ten years out here. We aren't as expendable as they'd like us to think." I closed my eyes. When I opened them again, night had fallen and the area silent.

Kira handed me a strip of dried meat. "It's not much."

"It'll be enough. Thank you." I got to my feet and glanced around at Lara who sat a few feet away from the rest of us with her husband. "We're moving out. Get her up. Keep her in the center of the circle if we have to fight." A fool or not, we couldn't lose anyone.

"I'll fight," Lara muttered. "I said I didn't want

to get torn to pieces."

After scouring our camp to make sure we didn't leave anything behind, I donned my rubber suit and led the others from our safe place. Fawke stepped to my side, taking the lead.

"Forget about your special assignment," I ordered. "If something happens to me, you'll have to lead these people. You're more valuable than I am."

"No way am I going to jeopardize not getting released on time." He shot me a glance. "Get used to it."

I squared my shoulders. "Are you disobeying a direct order?"

"Yes, ma'am." He gave me a sarcastic salute, then put his finger to his lips.

The rattling of wheels over stone and concrete the only sound as we traveled. When we reached the pass through, we spent too much time clearing the way to make room for the wagons. By the time we'd finished, sweat poured down my back inside the suit.

"A fifteen-minute break," I said, collapsing on a cement block tossed to the side. It could be the end of my ten years before we reached the far away mountain.

After ten minutes, I motioned for Fawke to come with me and marched to where our latest arrival had been attacked. Thankfully, the light from my headlight kept the carnage from being as stark as it would have been in the light of day.

Shreds of clothing and a few bones were all that was left of the poor girl. Her backpack yielded another long-range rifle and some food we could add to our stores. Her inexperience showed in the fact she'd chosen perishable items. Still, the couple pieces of fruit and the loaf of bread would be enjoyed by all, even if we only got a bite each.

"Nice score," Fawke said. "My mouth is watering in anticipation of those apples."

"I'd hoped for weapons." Knowing he'd take the pack anyway, I handed it to him.

He slung it over his shoulder and gave a shrill whistle, calling the others to join us with the wagons. While we waited, he cut the two apples into the right amount of slices. "We'll hold the bread to dunk into our soupy breakfast."

"Sounds fine to me." I accepted my slice, savoring the juicy sweetness on my tongue. Surprise that Soriah would offer such a luxury in the supply room rose. Yes, they'd sent chocolate once, and a pear, but it still seemed out of character. Unless they knew we'd derive strength from the gesture.

Moans arose from the others as they savored their treat, smiles gracing their faces. I'd like to see more happiness, something in very short supply in our dark and dangerous world. When they'd finished, I urged them on. We had a lot of ground to cover before morning and needed to find a place to hole up once the Malignants started to stir.

A stiff breeze kicked up dry grass, swirling it around us. A few times, they'd blow on one of the fires, then lift, burning orange, into the night sky, the only hint of color other than black and gray and the oranges and yellows of the gas fires.

Lara tripped and yelped before being helped by Shane. I rolled my eyes and shook my head. At least she could cook the unappetizing gruel that filled our bellies.

"Careful about showing your feelings for Lara on your face," Fawke said. "She's insecure as it is."

Remorse slumped my shoulders. "I know. I try, but she's more of a hindrance than a help. Even I did better when I arrived."

"Because you're one in a million." He bumped me playfully. "The others have started taking their cues from your behavior. I overheard Gage berating her for using too much water in the gruel."

"We shouldn't waste water."

"That's not my point, Crynn."

I sighed. "I know, and you're right. I'll do better. I promise." We were all in this together, able to fight or not. It would do me well to remember that fact.

16

It took two days to pull the wagons down the street. Two days full of fighting, bone-numbing exhaustion, and bloody hands as we continued to move obstacles out of our way.

At least traveling at night kept the numbers of Malignants to a minimum but the further we traveled, the more we started to see. We couldn't go more than a couple of blocks before being attacked by at least five of the beasts.

"This is going to take a very long time." Kira leaned heavily on the wagon. "We don't make five miles a day."

I agreed. The mountain seemed to get farther away instead of closer. "Today's Sunday. We'll wait for the drop here." I stared down a cracked street full of abandoned vehicles. A few buildings had toppled adding to the piles of stuff to be cleared. I grew more tired thinking of the work.

The rasp of stone against metal mingled with the

groans of our weary group as Fawke sharpened his sword. He motioned for me to lay my sword next to him. Too tired to tell him I could do it myself, I set it on the ground then pulled my container of black paint from my bag.

"Since we now know the chips won't kill us, why don't you wipe those black stripes off your face instead of reapplying them?" Ezra asked, headed for the sleeping wagon.

I shrugged. "I've gotten used to them." They'd actually become a sort of badge to me to remind me of who I am now. The old Crynn seemed like a stranger.

"He's right," Fawke said. "We wouldn't have to wear the scarves if you didn't paint the stripes."

"I like the scarf. It cuts down on the stench." Not to mention the odor of the constantly burning gas fires.

"Hides part of your pretty face." He grinned and continued sharpening.

He thought I was pretty? I ducked my head so he wouldn't see the blush I knew colored my face. I'd never cared what a man thought about me before. It didn't do anyone any good to form romantic relationships until they knew what fate the wheel decided for them. Now, here I was, with a job that didn't invite romance. At least not in my near future.

I bent my knees and wrapped my arms around them. What I wanted was sleep, but there'd be little of that. We'd need more than two people to fetch the crate when it arrived. Would another unlucky eighteen-year-old arrive with it?

Seeing the chopper in the distance, I got to my

feet. At least we wouldn't have to travel far. The road in front of us provided the perfect drop.

A few buildings down, three men stepped from a building. "We have company."

Fawke stood. "They're after the drop. Up everyone. Weapons in hand. We can't let them beat us to it." He tossed me my sword.

I caught it. "Shane and Lara stay behind and guard the supplies."

Without waiting for confirmation, I led the group at a run to where the crate started to fall. The strangers also sprinted toward the supplies. I raised my gun and fired a few feet in front of them.

They faltered but kept going as if they knew I didn't want to shoot them.

"I don't have a problem with it." Ezra took aim, shooting one of them in the leg.

His comrades took the screaming man by the arm and tried to drag him away. I shot again. "Drop him." I had some questions to ask the man. "Ezra, Dante, get the crate."

The two men ran in the opposite direction as Malignants raced toward us. Fawke and I raced to reach the fallen man before the creatures did. When we reached him, we hoisted him on our shoulders and half-ran, half-dragged him back to the others.

"Stop screaming or I'll finish the job." I pushed his arm off my shoulders and pulled my sword.

The others formed a fighting circle around the crate, except for Kira, who bound the man's leg. It didn't take us long to finish off the small group of Malignants.

"Thanks for not shooting to kill," I told Ezra.

"Figured you wanted to know more about this group we're after." He tossed the man over his shoulder, leaving Jolt to take his place in carrying the crate, and jogged back to the wagons.

By the time the rest of us joined them, he had the man tied to the wheel and Lara worked on cleaning his wound. "It's only a graze," she said. "He'll live."

"Of course, he will." Ezra scowled. "If I wanted him dead, he would be." He grabbed a crowbar and pried open the crate. "More oats, more water purification pills, a few medical supplies, no luxury items." He spit. "Not even a weapon or extra blankets. Soriah is getting stingy."

I still had the pack I wanted to barter with, but wanted to hold onto it until we needed something very badly. "We've survived this long. Maybe we'll run across another scavenger." I turned to our prisoner.

"Who are you?"

"I'm not talking."

I put the tip of my sword to his throat. "Then we have no reason to keep you alive."

"Fine. I'm a scout. Name is Rob."

"From the mountain?" I pressed the tip a tad tighter against his skin.

"Yes. My buddies will come for me."

"I doubt it. They ran off pretty fast to be loyal to you."

"That's because of those things. Not you." He spit at my feet.

Ezra kicked him. "Don't talk to our leader that way."

The man's eyes widened. "Leader? You're

barely out of diapers."

"She's mean enough to end your miserable life."

I put up a hand to stop Ezra from kicking Rob again. "How many of you are there?"

"In the city?"

"No. On the mountain."

He shrugged. "Never counted, but there's a lot. Women, children, fighters. If that's where you're headed, you'll never make it. You'll be picked off before you get close."

I glanced at Fawke. Was it possible a large group of people could thrive outside of Soriah? Was that the threat to our president? I motioned for Fawke to join me off to the side.

"What does President Cane expect us to do against an entire community?"

"Maybe we're only to locate them. Confirm they exist."

"Then what?" I frowned. "Continue the wasteful job of fighting Malignants? That's a battle we'll win. We'll never rid the world of those things." It didn't make sense. "What if we're disposable after finding this group of survivors?"

A stricken look crossed his face. "I hadn't thought of that."

"So, it's a possibility?"

"With Soriah, anything is possible."

I glanced at the rest of my group. All people unlucky enough to be sent here. Until we'd started seeing other people, I really did think our job was to fight Malignants until the end of our time here. Now, I wasn't so sure. Neither was I in a hurry to reach the mountain anymore.

I stepped away from the others and stared at the mountain rising in the distance. Trees dotted the landscape. Not as thick as I'd seen in some pictures, but some variant had struggled and survived. What other resources were there?

Was my life back in Soriah, on the mountain, or would I die in this city? Forbidden tears blurred my vision as confusion and fear clouded my mind. I swiped the back of my hand across my face and turned back to the prisoner.

"Where's your camp?"

"I can't tell you that. You'll attack."

"What are you doing in the city?"

"Looking for supplies."

"After all these years?" I frowned.

He shrugged. "The scavengers for that city you're from finds things."

"What do you need with luxuries?"

"We can use them to trade when Soriah comes."

I stared down at him. His community knew President Cane was searching for them. Would the president eradicate them all? Something about this man's people frightened those on the hill. I needed to find out what that fear was. It could be the leverage we needed in order not to be expendable.

"Everyone get some rest. We move out at dark." As usual, I took first watch, not caring who joined me. Of course, it was Fawke since he refused to relinquish his role as my protector. "Who's going to watch over me when you're gone?" I tilted my head.

"I'm sure Sharon will appoint someone else."

"What makes me so special?"

"Every group of people needs a leader." He gave

a crooked smile. "Otherwise, chaos reigns."

I snorted. "I could have been the world's worst choice for a leader."

"We got lucky."

We laughed and sat on some cement blocks, watching for signs of Malignants or humans. "What do we do with Rob?" I asked. "With a thriving community free from Soriah's eye, I doubt he'll want to join us."

"He won't be chipped, most likely."

I glanced at my right forearm. What would happen if I were to cut the chip out? Would Sharon think me dead? Did I want that? Without it, no supplies would be dropped. I doubted I'd survive the city without Soriah's help. I sighed and lowered my arm.

"What Rob has sounds enticing, doesn't it?"

I nodded. "I've never questioned the way the president ran things until now. It's the way it's been for a hundred years. Now, I question everything."

"That's because you have a good head on your shoulders." He put his arm around me, pulling me close.

Strange how right the gesture felt. His presence made me feel safe like nothing else could. I relaxed and leaned my head against him, giving into the pleasure of his touch for a moment.

"Hey, boss." Jolt joined us. "Rob is gone."

I bolted to my feet. "How is that possible? Was no one watching him?"

"Lara was supposed to be. She left him alone to go fix dinner. He rubbed his bindings against the wagon wheel." He held up the tattered remnants of a rope.

"Someone should have relieved Lara." I gritted my teeth and glanced at the wagon.

Rob could only have ducked into the nearest building. He wouldn't still be there. Now, we might not ever find his camp.

"What's the plan now?" Ezra crossed his arms. "We still heading to the mountain?"

"What choice do we have? If we don't do what we're told, there'll be no more supplies." I slumped against the wagon.

"What you're saying is that we keep on with this ridiculous quest." Gage smirked. "Endlessly walking and fighting until Rob's people, or the Malignants, kill us off."

"We'll come up with a plan." Fawke's tone left no room for argument. "For now, we keep moving forward."

Gage's face darkened. Scowling, she marched to the sleeping wagon and climbed into the tent.

"I'm with her," Dante said. "This aimless wandering is driving me nuts."

"It wasn't aimless until now," I said.

"Our mission was to find out if there were survivors. We've done that." His brow furrowed. "Why not inform Sharon? Maybe they'll let us all go home."

"Idiot." Ezra bopped him in the back of the head. "Do you really think they will? Not a chance. When we're no longer needed, Soriah will execute us all. I say we keep our mouth shut for now."

"I agree." The less those on the hill know, the better it is for us.

17

One of the wagon wheels started shaking halfway through the night. I found a cleared path between two buildings and told the others we'd camp there long enough to fix the wheel. I stepped through first, before Fawke could stop me and stopped short.

In front of me lay the smoldering remains of a campfire and a man curled up in a blanket fast asleep. A pile of supplies lay a few feet away. I pulled my sword and tapped him with it as Fawke joined me. "Looks like we found the scouts' camp."

"Yep." Fawke kicked the man's foot. "He isn't much of a guard."

The man's eyes sprang open, and he fought to untangle himself from his bedding. "What?" Once free, he sprang to his feet and reached for a dagger.

"Hold it right there." I kept my sword at the ready. "That little thing is no match for my sword. Where are your comrades?"

"Out scouting. You must be the people that shot

Rob." He paled and held up his hands. "I don't want any trouble."

"What are you scouting for?" Fawke asked, his eyes narrowing.

"Threats and supplies." He stepped in front of what he should have been guarding. "Don't take this. It's ours."

By now the others had joined us. With curious glances at the stranger, Dante and Jolt set to work fixing the wagon wheel.

"You folks seemed headed somewhere," the man said. "Mind telling me where?"

"Out of the city." He didn't need to know more than that.

He nodded. "Wanting to get away from those things, I guess." He sat on a pack lying on the ground. "Fix your wagon and get out of here before my friends return."

"I'm pretty sure we can handle them," Fawke said. "How many of you are there?"

He looked reluctant to answer, but after a minute shrugged. "You'd find out soon enough if you stick around long enough. There's only five now. Scavengers and monsters finished off the others. You scavengers?"

"Stalkers." I sheathed my sword. "It's our job to clear the city of Malignants. Since that is an impossible task, we're looking for a career change."

His eyes widened. "Soriah will kill you."

"If they find us." I glanced at Ezra whose mouth fell open and gave a slight shake of my head, hoping he'd play along. If we could convince the scouts we meant them no harm, we might find out the location of their home on the mountain. This lone scout didn't seem very bright, but he was talkative.

"Want me to go through the packs?" Ezra glared at the man who paled.

"No. We only take what we find left behind. We aren't thieves." Might not be my brightest idea, but these scouts should not be our enemies. I had a feeling we might need each other in the future. This group of people had escaped Soriah for years. I wanted to know their secret.

Suddenly feeling many years older than my eighteen years, I sat on the edge of the supply wagon. On the other side of the building came the shrieks of Malignants. The sound had become so familiar I no longer jerked or grabbed for my weapons. Not until I actually lay eyes on one.

The radio crackled.

"No one mention this man." I got to my feet and stood in front of the monitor as Sharon's face appeared.

"The Wheel did not land on black today."

"Okay." Why did she call to tell me something I'd figure out myself when no one arrived? "The president has decided to up your rations each week in order to give you the strength to continue hunting for survivors."

I fought the urge to glance at the man off to my side. "That's very nice of our president."

"President Cane is hoping for a quick end to this mission, Miss Dayholt. I hope you can oblige."

"We're doing our best. Pulling these wagons is slow going. The city is blocked every way we turn."

"I cannot send you more people." The screen

went black.

"I've never known Soriah to contact us about people not hitting the black square." Ezra shook his head. "For some reason, they want on your good side."

"Could they be suspicious that we're veering off their original plan for us?" I glanced at him.

"I don't know how. Not with these trackers in our arms. They know where we are at every turn."

"You have trackers?" The scout's brows disappeared under his cap.

"Yeah, so?" I stared.

"Nothing." He looked worried.

Fawke motioned his head for me to step away from the others. "The closer we get to finding this mountain community, the greater the risk to them. Soriah will know their location by our trackers. Until we know whether these people are actually a threat to the city, we can't lead them there."

"I know that. Any ideas how to prevent it from happening?"

"Short of cutting the chips from our arms, no." He exhaled heavily. "We've a lot of thinking to do. I'm so close to my release date. Ridding myself of my tracker means I never go back."

"We won't let that happen. I'll think of something. A story you can tell. Make it look as if the rest of us have died at the hands of Malignants."

His gaze locked on mine. "You'd do that for me?"

"If that's what I decide, yes." Without hesitation. Fawke had almost served his term. He'd be a huge asset to Soriah in some way.

I paced away from the others, deep in my thoughts. Kira and Ezra would jump at the chance of freedom. Anyone who wanted to join the mountain people…I'd find a way to make that happen. As for me, well, I hadn't totally decided my fate. Perhaps I'd continue to hole up and wait out my time.

The city would continue to send me rations. Others would spin the wheel and land on black. I'd learned to fight, and if I ventured out only at night, then perhaps I'd survive. Yes. When we got close to finding the mountain community, I'd let each of my group make their own decision.

"Wagons fixed." Dante wiped his hands on a rag.

"Let's go. We need to find a place to hide out before daylight." I glanced at the dumbfounded scout. "Take care of yourself. It's best to travel at night when the beasts are less active."

"Thanks. You, too."

We headed away from the camp as five men, sending curious looks our way, sprinted to their comrade. I smiled knowing they feared the worst, but that they'd find him alive and well. We were here to kill monsters, not people.

"I don't understand what's going on?" Gage fell into step beside me, her face creased with confusion, fear, and a bit of anger. "As our leader, it's your duty to keep us updated on your plans."

"I'm still working that out."

"We're going to reach that mountain. Then what?"

"I said I'm working on it." I increased my pace.

"Trouble?" Fawke took Gage's place at my side.

"A bit. I don't know what to tell people. We

might not live to make it to the mountain. With scouts, scavengers, and Malignants, the fighting will only increase. When we get close, I'll have a plan. The group needs to trust me." Trying to work out what was best for everyone gave me a headache.

Again, I let hatred for the wheel and everything Soriah rise up. Why had I had such bad luck as to be the new leader? I'd prefer someone else make the decisions for the group. Stalker my hide. We were nothing but spies and wanderers.

"Hey!" A shout came from behind us.

Fawke and I whirled, guns raised, as two men raced toward us. "That's close enough," Fawke said.

"We have a proposition," one said.

"We're listening."

"Our friend told us how you didn't harm him or steal our things. How about we join forces until we reach the city's edge? Strength in numbers, you know?"

I glanced at Fawke. We hadn't harmed their friend, but that didn't mean we could trust them.

"As the leader, it's your call," he said.

"What do you think?"

"It's a risk, but he has a point. The closer we get to the city's center, the thicker the Malignants."

And I did say I wanted more people. "Okay. We're looking for a place to camp for the day. Catch up to us."

"Thanks." They turned and darted away.

Their shouts pulled a few Malignants from the shadows. Fawke's and my guns finished them off easily enough.

We were blocked by another toppled building.

More fires burned the closer we got to the center, filling the air with the stinging odor of gas.

"I guess we're spending the day here." I hated the openness. I scanned the buildings closest to us. "Fawke, maybe we can stay in that one." I pointed to a four-story building that showed promise. At least we'd be out of the open.

"The wagons won't fit."

"We'll place guards. Malignants won't steal our supplies, and a couple of guards can alert the rest of us if scavengers show up."

"Let's check it out." He led the way into the dark.

When we didn't find anything to alarm us, we told the others we'd camp there. As was the norm, Fawke and I took the first watch. I hoped the scouts showed up soon. Other members of our group might shoot first and ask questions later.

I leaned against the wagon and trained my gaze on the road in front of us. The weak sun blocked by gray clouds failed to pierce the gloom. I missed the fake sunshine of Soriah.

"The longer you're here, the more glum you get." Fawke's worried gaze settled on my face.

"That's because for every obstacle we climb over, there's more, and I'm not talking just about finding a way over buildings and around rusted vehicles from a century ago."

"I've told you many times what a good head you have on your shoulders. You'll make the right choices."

I shot him a quick glance. "Will I? I'm not sure I can continue under the pressure."

"You can, and you will. We've seen more

cooperation from Soriah under your charge than ever before. They see the value in you. Now, you need to see your own value."

I smirked. If I went through with the idea I toyed with in my mind, I'd become a rebel. One of the very people we hunted for. My mother would be mortified and shunned. Would my freedom be worth that? Only if I could find a way to free the people of Soriah from President Cane's rule.

I rolled my head on my shoulders, trying to release the kinks caused by stress. In the growing light of day, I spotted the scouts coming our way and prayed I hadn't made a bad decision by allowing them to temporarily join us.

"Hard to get the wagons around this." A burly man I guessed was their leader, motioned to the wall.

"It is. We'll spend half the night trying to clear a path."

"Why not ditch the wagons?"

"We have supplies and a tent. We can't always find a place to sleep out of the acid rain."

He shrugged. "We manage. Name's Lloyd."

"Crynn Dayholt. This is Fawke."

"Closed spaces are claustrophobic," he said. "We'll sleep under your wagon." He tossed his back in and climbed under, the other four following.

It relieved some of my worry to know they wouldn't be sharing my group's sleeping quarters. Two guards at a time could guarantee these men didn't try to steal our supplies.

We now had five extra pairs of hands to move debris. Our travels would be easier for however long we traveled together.

All I had to do was keep them a secret from Soriah.

18

When we woke that evening, the scouts were gone. I glared at Shane and Lara. "What happened? You were on watch."

"We fell asleep." Embarrassment flickered across Shane's face. "Lara isn't feeling well."

"What's wrong with her?" Kira placed the back of her hand across the other woman's forehead. "She's hot."

"I don't think I sterilized some water I drank good enough." Perspiration dotted Lara's upper lip.

"You know the dangers of this place." I gritted my teeth to keep from saying something I'd regret. "We can't afford to have anyone down. Now, the scouts are gone. Most likely to alert their comrades to our presence."

"If they don't already know," Fawke said. "I think they wanted safety in numbers to get a good night's sleep. There doesn't appear to be any supplies missing."

"Thank the Supreme Being for that." I marched away from the group, clenching my fists hard enough for my fingernails to dig into my palms.

Why didn't Shane keep better watch over his wife? Did the woman have a death sentence?

I stared down the crowded street. From the best of my calculations, we were in the city center. A few more days of travel and we'd be out. What waited for us out there?

Ezra didn't think the Malignants roamed the open lands, preferring the dark damp of abandoned buildings to pastureland, once fertile, now nothing but miles of dried weeds. Still, there was something out there that helped an entire community survive.

"Are you okay?" Fawke placed a hand on my shoulder.

"I'd like to kill something."

He laughed. "Maybe you'll get lucky, and a Malignant will venture from its lair."

"How messed up is that?" I grinned. "Hoping for one of those things to attack?"

"We could have a sparring session to allow everyone to work off some steam."

"As tempting as that is, we need our strength for the journey." I wanted to rest my cheek on his hand, have him pull me into a hug, smooth the hair from my face like my mother would do when I was sick or feeling bad. Instead, I squared my shoulders and stepped away.

Lara leaned heavily on her husband as we made our way slowly down the street full of potholes. More fires than I'd seen before burned in the cracked asphalt, taking away the chill of the night. With no rain in sight, and not being attacked by a horde, we rarely wore our rubber suits unless going out during the day.

Another good thing about more fires is less Malignants. I would have thought the hairless creatures would relish the heat, but they seemed to prefer the cold.

Something clattered in an alley to my right. I held up my hand to stop the group. When the sound didn't come again, I waved everyone forward. We didn't get far before I heard it again.

"What is that?" I asked.

"No idea." Fawke pulled his sword. "I'll go check it out."

Not without me. I gripped my own weapon and followed.

Halfway down the alley I spotted what caused the racket. An injured Malignant fought to stand on a leg sporting a huge gash. "I think the scouts had gone through here. Why didn't they finish the creature off?" With one swipe of my sword, I took off its head.

"Feel better?" Fawke flashed a grin. "You killed something."

"Very funny." I stood and stared at the four-story building. No faces appeared at any of the broken windows. Why injure a Malignant and leave it for us to find? I whirled, eyes wide. "The scouts left it to lure us here. They're after the supplies."

We sprinted back to the others, alerting them to get ready.

"Look." I pointed to a window on the top floor of the building across from us.

A man hung out the window.

A Malignant shrieked.

The man, one of the scouts from last night, jumped. He landed with the sound of a melon hitting cement.

I rushed forward, Kira and Fawke at my side. He'd been gutted. "I guess he jumped to keep from being torn apart further," I said, grimacing. Not that I blamed him.

The largest number of Malignants we'd run across yet spewed from the building. The scouts hadn't left a trap, they had. "Run!"

The three of us turned and sprinted back to the others and formed our fighting circle. The injured Malignant must have had something wrong with it and the others left it as bait. Either that or the scout who'd jumped had gotten a good swing in before being hurt himself. Despite living among them as long as I had, I didn't know enough about them to know the answer.

Shrieks filled the air, along with the rotten odor of the monsters. I pulled my scarf over my nose and mouth to make breathing a little easier and aimed my gun.

Guns fired, picking off a good number of the attackers before they got close enough for hand-to-hand combat. I set my gun on the ground and pulled my sword. "Do not step in front of me," I told Fawke. "We fight side-by-side." My tone left no room for argument. His special assignment be damned.

I dropped to one knee and thrust upward, stabbing a Malignant in the stomach. I withdrew, stood, and whirled, decapitating it as I had the one in the alley. Then, I turned and swiped as another charged.

Lara screamed behind me.

I barely got a glimpse of the Malignant biting into her neck before Shane killed it, only to be set upon by two more. We were losing the battle. "Do not let down your guard!"

Exhaustion slowed my movements. Still, I kept fighting. Behind me came the pants and grunts of my friends.

"We've got watchers," Fawke said. "Two o'clock."

I spared a glance to see the scouts watching but making no move to help us. They probably hoped we would die at the hands of the Malignants so they could take our supplies. Not today. I fought like a dervish, forcing my tired arms to continue, until the last Malignant lay dead and blood coated my arms and clothing. I gave Lloyd a jaunty salute, then turned away as the scouts melted into the shadows.

"Lara's dead," Kira said, "and Shane won't last long. She didn't have the strength to fight, her being ill."

My heart lurched. "Anyone else injured?"

She shook her head.

"What happens if someone is bitten? Will they die?"

"No. But they will get sick enough to wish they did." Kira pushed to her feet. "The poison lasts three to five days before our bodies fight it off. Lara died because her jugular was punctured. Shane's been gutted."

I stood over him. "I'm so sorry."

His gaze fixed on my face. "She didn't want to go on without our babies. This way is good enough for me." His eyes closed, and his breathing shallowed until he passed.

"Wash up and move out." I closed my eyes and said a prayer for the two we'd lost. I almost expected a call from Sharon, but none came. The loss of two petty thieves wouldn't matter much to Soriah.

Jolt and Dante dragged the bodies to one of the fires and lay them across it. We stood and paid silent respects as we wiped the blood from our exposed skin. When we'd finished, we set off again, a silent and subdued group.

I kept everyone going, farther than we usually did, wanting to leave the place our comrades had fallen as far behind us as possible. Every bad thought I'd had about Lara rose up and threatened to choke me. This time I ignored Alga's words and let the cleansing tears flow.

Fawke sent some concerned glances my way, but didn't talk. His presence was enough. I knew he felt the loss as keenly as I did.

When I felt none of us could go any further, I called a halt in a shelled out building. The front had fallen, leaving three walls intact. With the wagons in front of us, it would provide a safe shelter. "No guards tonight. Everyone needs a full day's sleep." We'd hear if someone came.

The day passed peacefully. I woke refreshed to the aroma of coffee. My eyes snapped open. "Where did that come from?"

Kira smiled and handed me a cup. "I found it in Lara's pack."

"Anything else good in there?" She'd told me she hadn't squirreled anything else away. For once, I was glad she lied.

"Enough coffee for us all to have another morning of enjoyment. That's it."

"I'll take it." Today was a good day to splurge.

The coffee seemed to raise everyone's spirits. For once, no one grumbled about the gruel we ate every morning. Smiles graced every face as we set off in the dark.

The closer we got to the city's edge, the fewer buildings and debris we had to find a way around. Buildings got shorter, some still in one piece. The stench of Malignants faded.

Again, I thought of the tracker in my arm. Soon, I'd have to make a critical decision, and I wasn't sure how the others would accept what I would offer them.

The radio crackled, and I called a halt. "Hello, Sharon."

"Pity about the husband and wife," she said.

"Their names were Shane and Lara."

She sighed. "We have a few more spinning the wheel tonight. Perhaps you'll get someone to take their place."

While we needed help, I didn't want anyone to suffer this life. "Some luxury items in our next drop would be nice."

"It never hurts to ask." A faint smile tugged at her lips. "You definitely keep me on my toes, Miss Dayholt." She signed off.

"I think she's keeping tabs on us," Ezra said. "She's never let us know of a wheel night before.

Someone either shows up or they don't. What does she think you're up to?"

"I'll let everyone know my thoughts in a day or two." I set off again. Presenting the offer could get me executed if one of my group was a hard believer of Soriah's ways.

I wasn't worried about the lifers or Fawke. He'd make the choice to stay. Gage worried me, though, because I still got hard looks when she didn't think I watched her. The more time I spent with Fawke, the more glares I got. Surely, she knows his plans on no attachments this close to his release.

Morning arrived earlier as we stepped out of the shadows of the city buildings. A large field of dead brush and grass stretched as far as the eye could see. I took a deep breath of air not rancid with Malignants or gas fires. Not as clean as the manufactured air of Soriah, but better than what we'd had before.

I glanced again at my arm. Tomorrow, I'd present the offer. Today, we'd rest. Maybe do some sparring, while we waited for the supply drop and to see whether anyone new arrived. If so, I'd have to decide how to handle them when I told the others of my plan. A newcomer might not be willing to stay.

Already, I missed my mother, knowing I might never see her again. I glanced at Fawke. I'd miss him, too. More than I cared to admit.

19

The others were more than happy to have a day of rest after days of fighting and clearing a path. Today, would most likely be our last day for a supply drop, not that I'd told the others yet. At least it would be my last day.

I'd pondered many times over the last few days on what my future held and it didn't include living under the strict rules of Soriah. My mother had once told me I had the heart of a rebel. I think she was more right than she knew. My heart ached at not seeing her again, and I prayed she wouldn't suffer repercussions of my actions. If things went right, she'd think me dead along with everyone else and would have the chance to grieve.

While the others sparred, I wandered the area not finding signs of any other living creature, four-legged or two. The tension that had become a part of me started to melt away.

Giggles, then a shriek of outrage, drew my

attention back to the others. Fawke had whacked Gage in the rear with his stick. His laughter caused my heart to jump.

Gage parried with a thrust to the stomach. Where before sparring had a serious tone, today's was playful.

A longing to join in consumed me only to be squelched. Some of them would hate me by morning. Some, like Ezra and Kira, even the former prisoners, might join me. A life on the mountain might be more preferable to them than the rest of their lives as Stalkers.

Fawke caught me watching and headed my way, leaving Gage with a petulant look on her face. With a toss of her ponytail, she marched to spar with Jolt.

"She's in love with you," I said.

"Nah, she loves any man. Craves male companionship. She's pretty enough, but her neediness turns people off." He studied my face so long, I turned my head. "You're leaving."

"You know what Soriah will require of us once we find the survivors. They'll kill everyone of us so words of hope that life out here is possible doesn't reach the poorest of Soriah. I can't be a part of that." I scuffed my foot in the dirt rather than meet his gaze.

"That might not happen." He sounded curt.

"But, it might. After almost ten years out here, are you willing to take that chance? They may not let you back."

"I've considered that." With his finger, he tilted my head up until our gazes locked. "I think I'm willing to take that chance. I've given them everything during my time. Two years more isn't such a hardship."

"But my ten years just started." I pulled away.

"Your mother—"

"Will think me dead. She'll be okay." I made a move to walk away, only to have him grab my arm. Over his shoulder, I noticed the others watching, concern and confusion on their faces.

"Your choice will have me failing my assignment for the second time."

"I'm sorry. That's one more reason for you to seriously think about your decision."

"Then now is the time to tell them." He pulled me back to the others. "Our leader has something to say." He gave me a push.

"I thought you agreed with my decision." I glared.

"At first, but now I see how foolish it is."

"What?" Ezra crossed his arms. "I know you've been pondering something for days. Something that involves every one of us. Your face always gives you away."

"I'm not going to remain under Soriah's control." I squared my shoulders and looked at each face in turn. "I'm going to fake my death."

"How?" Riva asked, her brow furrowed.

"By cutting out my tracker and letting them think me dead."

"Why?" Moses shook his head. "It's insane."

"Soriah will want us to find the rebels. They'll know their location by our trackers. After that, we're all expendable." I lifted my chin.

"You think they'll kill us before attacking the rebels," Ezra said.

"I do. This is a decision each of you must make for yourself. Once I've removed my tracker, I'm going to ask the mountain community to allow me refuge." I stood there, still as stone while the others conversed among themselves.

After several long minutes, Ezra spoke. "We'd like today to think about which path we choose."

"I agree. It's an important decision, and not one to be taken likely." With a harsh glare at Fawke for forcing my hand, I headed across the expanse of dead grass to find solitude and wait for the supply drop. For once Fawke didn't seek me out. I figured he was discussing the news I'd dropped with the others.

I glanced up as a chopper circled. A few seconds later, the white of a parachute shined in the gray sky. Without the threat of Malignants, I got to my feet and strolled toward the drop. I grasped one handle and started dragging it back to camp. Seeing my struggle, Dante raced to help.

"I'm coming with you," he said. "I don't need to think it over."

"You're close to release time. Are you sure?"

"I've nothing waiting for me in Soriah."

"Except a life of luxury."

"If they don't kill me as you said." He grinned, his teeth flashing against his dark skin. "Besides, a life of luxury will make me fat and lazy."

I laughed. "I'll be glad to have you with me."

"Who knows? Maybe my charm will win you over, and you'll have my babies." He winked and gave a cheeky grin.

My laughter increased, attracting the attention of the rest of our group. With serious expressions, they watched as Dante and I carried the crate to them.

"What about our supplies?" Kira asked.

"We'll split it evenly among those who stay and those who go." I was still their leader as long as the chip remained under my skin.

Ezra pried open the crate revealing our usual supplies along with coffee, two loaves of bread, and something in a jar. "What's that?"

Lotus smiled. "That's a butter to spread on bread. It's made from berries and nuts." She rubbed her hands together.

"Let's have us a feast," I said. People thought better when relaxed with a full belly.

Kira made coffee and sliced the bread, handing each of us a slice slathered with the brown spread. "We probably should have saved one of the loaves, but what the heck. We're splitting up soon anyway."

"I've made my choice." Dante took a big bite. "I'm going with Crynn. I would have a hard time adjusting to that lifestyle after nine years out here."

"Look." Gage pointed as another chopper appeared.

Two people jumped out. I groaned. Newcomers could put a kink in my plan.

"Guess you've got to explain to two more how you're turning rebel." Fawke narrowed his eyes.

I shrugged. The newcomers might be the easiest to convince since they'd still be shocked about the wheel landing on black. "No need to meet them. No Malignants to attack. Let them come to us."

"All I have left of the bread is the hard ends," Kira said.

"They'll be glad of it." I finished my slice and

wiped my hands on my leather skirt, then got to my feet to stand and greet the newcomers.

Two males, identical twins, approached us. I turned to Ezra. "Has this ever happened before?"

"Not that I know of."

"Poor fools." Moses shook his head. "Well, I reckon I've made my choice, too, Crynn. I'm a lifer. What have I got to lose? I'll be joining you."

"As will I." Ezra nodded.

"Me, too," Kira said. "We're stuck here no matter what."

"I don't want to stay here." Gage glanced up, her expression grave. "I've nine more years. How will I survive out here alone?"

"Fawke's staying," I said, knowing that would cement her decision. "Maybe these twins will, too."

"Great. Two who can't fight." She licked her fingers and glanced at the radio.

"Don't," Fawke said. "Don't betray those you've fought alongside by calling Sharon."

"Whatever." She pasted on a smile as the twins joined us.

"Welcome. I'm Crynn Dayholt, the leader. Make yourselves comfortable." I'd let them settle in a while before letting them know what was going on.

"Ted and Ned. Guess you know why we're here. I'm Ted, in gray. Ned wears black." They both accepted the bread from Kira.

"Why don't you have any weapons?" I tilted my head.

"We spun the wheel, ate a big meal, and got flown out the next morning. We were able to grab a few food items." Ted shrugged out of his pack and handed it to me.

"It was weird," his brother said. "I spun first, the needle landing on black. Some old hag said since we're twins, the decision counted for us both."

I raised my brows at Fawke. He shrugged, but didn't say anything.

These two were Shane and Lara's replacements. Those in charge waited for an opportunity to replace them, knowing we'd have held onto their weapons. Hope rose in me. This meant they had no idea what I planned to do.

Talk returned to plans of staying and going. Gage was more than happy to explain to the twins.

They glanced at me in alarm. "The chips," Ted said.

"Won't kill us," I answered. "We've tested them."

"Monsters?"

"Back there." I jerked my thumb over my shoulder. "They don't like open spaces."

"So, if we go with you we won't have to fight them?" A hopeful expression crossed Ned's face. "We were told about them by the pilot right before he told us to jump."

"I can't promise you that. Just be glad you didn't have to fight your way to us. You don't have to make your decision now."

"It's an easy one. We've been orphans since the age of ten. We're staying." Ned glanced at his brother who nodded. "No one will miss us when we die, real death or fake."

Fawke made a noise in his throat and marched away.

My heart sank. With every person who made the decision to follow me, left him with one less fighter. He'd return to danger of the burning city with a much smaller group. If I knew him as well as I thought I did, he'd return even if he returned alone.

"Let him be," I said when Gage made a move to follow him.

"You are no longer my leader." She planted her fists on her hips.

"I am as long as this chip is in my arm." I narrowed my eyes. "If you go now, you'll make him resentful. Learn to read his body language if you plan on spending the next two years with him."

Face darkening, she climbed into the tent like a pouting teenager. I sighed and shook my head, hoping she'd listen to Ezra and not contact Sharon. If she did, the life of every person who said they'd follow me would be forfeit. Our deaths ordered.

Fawke might hesitate if told to kill us, but Gage wouldn't spare a second thought at getting rid of me. I exhaled heavily. "I need everyone's decision by night fall."

"The three of us will go," Riva said. "We've nothing back there. Once they released us from prison, we knew we were here for life."

That left only Fawke and Gage, the two survivors of our group, to explain to Sharon what had befallen us. I nodded, wondering whether he'd blame our deaths on Malignants or the survival group.

"Formation!" I grabbed my weapons as a large group of men and women sprinted toward us.

Fawke dashed back to my side. "You're still my assignment as long as you have your chip."

I smiled and raised my weapon. "Do not fire unless fired upon. They may be friendly." A fact confirmed a minute later as they waved a white flag.

Lowering my gun, I held up my hand, recognizing Lloyd leading the group. His unsmiling face had me raising my weapon again.

Too late. We were outnumbered two-to-one. The survivors formed a circle around us.

CYNTHIA MELTON

20

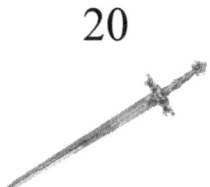

"Drop your weapons," Lloyd said. "You won't win this fight."

"We didn't harm your man." I glared as my weapons were taken, and my hands tied behind my back. "Why repay us this way?"

"Our leader wants to meet with you." He motioned for a man with a knife to step forward.

Before I knew what was happening, he'd cut the chip from my arm and crushed it under his boot. I gritted my teeth against the pain as he moved from one of my group to the other doing the same.

"Guess the decision of whether to go or stay was made for me." Fawke's face darkened.

"I'm sorry." I blinked back the tears wanting to spring forth. "I didn't plan this."

Gage screamed as they cut her, making things worse as she struggled. Stupid girl. If she didn't stop fighting, she'd be cut too deep and bleed to death.

"Stop." Fawke must have thought the same thing.

"Squirming is only going to hurt you."

"So, we're all basically dead?" Riva frowned as one of the scouts wrapped a rag around her cut.

"Yeah." I winced as my bandage was tightened. At least that was what I hoped Soriah would know.

Lloyd shot the radio with my gun. It flew off the wagon and lay smoldering in the weeds. "You won't need that where we're going."

"Where are we going?"

"Up there. We've got quite a hike." He turned and headed away from the city, leaving the others to keep my group in a tight cluster.

We should never have let our guard down. Guilt ripped a hole in my chest. I'd foolishly thought us safe since the Malignants didn't venture out. How wrong I'd been. I hung my head and trudged along, feeling lonelier than ever without Fawke trying to raise my spirits as usual.

I gave him a sideways glance. A muscle ticked in his jaw as he stared straight ahead. I sighed and followed, trying to ignore the throbbing in my arm.

Would Sharon believe a group our size would have no survivors? I wouldn't. Half maybe, but not this many. I glanced over my shoulder, the ruined radio too far now to see, but would it have been better to leave it intact? Of course, if Sharon called and didn't see bodies…

What did the community's leader want with us? Would we be tortured and killed for information about Soriah and President Cane?

"Act like the leader you are," Fawke hissed. "Hold your head up. Don't show weakness."

"So, you're talking to me now?"

He exhaled sharply through his nose. "This isn't your fault. Bad luck. That's all. Maybe it's the Supreme Being's plan for me to leave Soriah. I can't tell the future."

"You're so good at adapting."

"A person has to out here." He didn't smile at me, his eyes didn't twinkle, but at least he spoke to me. I'd take what I could get.

Deciding to resume my role as leader, I squared my shoulders and pushed through the men surrounding us to reach Lloyd. "What does your leader want with us?"

"To talk."

"When you joined us the other night, then left, was this the plan all along?"

He laughed. "Pretty smart, huh? Act all friendly, get you to let down your guard, then swoop in, taking you and the supplies."

"Your leader doesn't know." The man lied.

"No, he doesn't, but he'll be as pleased as someone who'd scored a piece of chocolate." Wrinkles spread from the corners of his eyes as he grinned. "We've taken a good number away from Soriah. Fighters. Oh, yes, he'll be happy about us bringing you all in."

"What will happen to us?"

"That depends on whether you pass the tests."

"What kind of tests?"

His laughter grew. "You won't like them, but they're entertaining for the community."

Dread sent rivulets of ice down my back. The very place I'd wanted to go might be the exact opposite of what I'd hoped. I wanted a peaceful place to live out my life, maybe have a family someday. Instead, I'd be used as entertainment. It didn't sound as if it would bode well for my group.

"I suppose you can't give me more information on these tests?"

"Nope. I'd rather it be a surprise." He laughed again and ordered me back to the group.

"What?" Fawke asked when I fell back into step next to him.

"We're going to be forced to some sort of test to determine our fate. Lloyd wouldn't tell me more than that."

Fawke frowned and stared at the back of Lloyd's head. "A fight?"

I shrugged. "Maybe a series of questions? We can speculate all we want, but until we arrive, we won't know anything."

"I don't like it."

Neither did I.

I moved to Lars and Dayton. "Have you had any experience with these people?"

"No. Scavengers stay in the city," Dayton said. "Maybe these people will send us back to scavenge for them. Or let us be scouts. We know the place really well."

Lars's eyes widened. "You'd be willing to go back where those things are?"

"If it meant staying alive and well in this so-called community. If we can't prove we have value to them, they'll get rid of us."

"No use speculating," Ezra said. "What will be will be. If they can't see the value in a group of trained fighters, then they can all kiss a Malignant's rear end."

Despite the seriousness of our situation, I couldn't hold in my laugh. "I'd like to see that."

He grinned. "It's only a matter of time before Soriah sends an army to our last known location. They'll find this mountain community. Lloyd's people will need fighters."

I now had the proposition I'd give the leader. Our skills for our lives.

By late afternoon, we left the openness of the fields and entered blackened pine trees. Somehow, the trees managed to survive the harshness of our world. No longer green like I'd seen in books, they still reached for the sky and littered the ground with needles. The further we went, the thicker they were.

I smiled and lifted my face heavenward. If only the sun would shine. Instead, clouds thickened, promising rain. I hoped we'd arrive at our destination before the poison fell from the sky.

Catching a glimpse of one of the scouts ogling Lotus, I moved to her side and sent him a warning glance. He chuckled. "You're just as pretty in my eyes. It's nice to have new blood arrive in female form."

"Keep your eyes and hands where they belong or you'll be missing one or two."

"I like my women feisty."

Fawke joined us, adding his glare to mine. "This one belongs to me."

The man shrugged. "There are others." He stepped a few feet away.

"I can handle myself," I said.

"I know, but as our leader…"

"Still keeping with your assignment?" I arched a brow.

"Hard habit to break."

"You're her bodyguard?" Lloyd glanced back. "Never heard of such a thing out here."

"He isn't." I shook my head. Fawke needed to stop putting himself between me and trouble. Doing so could have severe consequences to him. "Stop. You might be putting a target on your back."

"We're here." Lloyd led us into a large clearing full of wood houses similar to what I'd lived in with my mother.

A worn dirt path cut the community in two. At the end sat a house twice the size of the others.

"Wait here." Lloyd left us under the curious gazes of a large number of men, women, and children.

I glanced around not seeing any expressions on their faces to alarm me. They merely stared, no doubt waiting to see what their leader would do.

A few minutes later, a man around Ezra's age, with gray hair and broad shoulders, approached us. He smiled. "I'm Jenkins, the leader of this group."

I stepped forward. "Crynn Dayholt, leader of this group."

Surprise flickered across his face. "Bad turn of the wheel, huh? Welcome to Rebel Village."

"Are we welcome here? It doesn't look that way to me, since our hands have been tied since we were captured." I lifted my chin to meet his gaze.

"Of course. Please untie her and the others. Provide them with food and water. We aren't barbarians. If you'd come with me Miss Dayholt."

He turned and entered the house he'd exited.

I motioned for Fawke to come with me, only to have him stopped by Lloyd.

"The boss will see you alone."

I took a deep breath and entered the building. A fire burned in a rock fireplace. On a small table sat a loaf of bread and a dented metal pitcher. A mouth-watering aroma came from a covered dish.

"Please, have something to eat." He handed me a bowl and lifted the lid.

"You have vegetables?" I widened my eyes. "I haven't seen any for a long time."

"I'll show you around. You'll be quite surprised by what we've accomplished away from Soriah." He filled the bowl with stew and handed it to me.

I almost moaned in ecstasy at the rich taste. "What kind of meat is this?" It didn't look like the manufactured stuff we got back home.

"Venison." He grinned. "Those monsters in the city would have a field day if they learned deer still roamed this mountain. We eat wild birds, rodents if we have to. The forest is coming back to life, Miss Dayholt."

"If Soriah finds out…" I dipped a piece of bread into my soup.

"We can't let that happen. That's why Lloyd cut the chips from your arms."

"I planned on it anyway." I glanced up from my meal. "I'd given my people the choice. Cut out their chips and come with me here or stay behind. Lloyd made that decision for all of us."

"Why did you want to come here?" He crossed his arms and leaned back in his chair.

"Same reason you're here. Freedom. Is this part of my test?"

"A small part." Something in his eyes made me squirm. "I see you have several young women of child-bearing years. I sincerely hope everyone passes the test."

"What is it?"

"Let's not talk of such things today. It will keep until tomorrow. Are you an educated woman?"

I nodded. "I read everything I can."

"Then you'll be even more surprised by what we've accomplished here." He stood as I finished eating. "Let's take that tour and have the cut on your arm cleaned."

"Our member, Kira, has some medical knowledge if she can be of help."

"We'll see."

A look of relief crossed Fawke's face as I stepped outside. I nodded to let him know I was fine.

Jenkins led me to a corral of deer. I'd seen something similar for cows and horses. A covered pen held pigeons, the only thing I'd actually seen in Soriah that wasn't a picture. Another building with slats for the roof held a garden.

"I am impressed. What about the rain?"

"The trees filter out the poison. Nature adapts, Miss Dayholt, much as humans can."

"You don't need to protect your skin?"

"Not here. I'm sure you saw how we're thriving, the amount of children we have. Rebel City is as close to paradise as one can find on this earth." His chest swelled.

"How did you do this?"

"Fifty years ago, my father and mother escaped Soriah. They were scavengers. They cut the chips from their arms and came to the mountain. Over time, they brought others here, same as Lloyd brought you. He had them pass a series of tests to prove their worthiness. You'll rarely find a scar now where a chip once was."

"What if a person doesn't pass the test?"

He shrugged. "We can't let them go back."

So, failure meant death.

21

After sleeping on a mattress stuffed with dry grass and eating more for breakfast than I normally ate in a full day, I stepped from the shack I shared with the other women in my group. In the center of the community, men erected what looked like an arena of some kind. Part of the testing, no doubt.

Jenkins strolled toward me, a smile on his face. "I trust you slept well."

"Better than I have in a long time."

"Wonderful. Please bring all members of your group here and have them line up. Your testing will begin."

"Before breakfast?" I tilted my head and smirked.

He gave a loud, bold laugh. "Cheeky one. I'll have something brought out to you. Today will be tiring. You'll need your strength."

Great. I stuck my head back in the shack and told the other women to meet me outside, then headed to the one next door and knocked. A shirtless Fawke answered. My mouth dried up at the sight of muscles and a wide array of scars across his chest.

"No sense sleeping fully clothed with no threat of Malignants." He grinned.

"Right. Uh. Our testing is about to begin. You and the others are to line up outside the shack next door." I whirled and rushed away before I made a fool of myself.

Breakfast was bread smeared with a tasty nut butter similar to our treat dropped by Soriah. I narrowed my eyes, wondering whether this had come from the supplies Jenkins had confiscated. I shrugged. Food was food.

When we'd finished, Jenkins, flanked by Lloyd and another man I didn't know, stood in front of us. "Ready, Miss Dayholt?"

I glanced at my group. "I guess so." Hard to answer when I didn't know what would be required of us."

"As your group's leader, the questions will be asked of you. It is up to you to determine the fate of your people." Instead of the friendly demeanor of this morning, Jenkins's face now looked carved from stone. "The others will not answer. They will not speak. If they do, they are forfeited. Understand?"

Everyone nodded. A muscle ticked in Fawke's jaw signaling his displeasure.

"We understand." I stood as straight as I could and met his gaze.

"How many under your command have you lost?"

"Two. To Malignants."

"Have you allowed others into your group that

were not sent by Soriah?"

"Yes. Two scavengers we captured." I motioned to Lars and Dayton. "We don't kill valuable people."

His eyes flashed. "Go down the line and tell me the value of each of your people and why I should allow them to stay."

Questions weren't so bad. I could do this all day. "Fawke is our best fighter and calm during a battle. Plus, he's young. Dante is strong as an ox and good at repairs. Gage is of breeding age and a good fighter. Moses is a good fighter with a good head on his shoulders. A sharp wit. Ezra has been here for a very long time and knows how to survive, not to mention his skill with a sword. Kira is young enough to bear children and is handy with injuries. Jolt is young and strong, getting better at fighting every day. Lars and Dayton, former scavengers, know the city inside and out. Riva, Samson, Jep, Lotus, and Zed are all survivors, strong, quick thinkers, and obedient. Ted and Ned are the newest members of our group, but learning fast."

"And you, Miss Dayholt? What is your worth?"

I swallowed against the boulder building in my throat. "I've kept these people alive long enough to find you."

His features relaxed as he laughed. "Not to mention humorous, beautiful, of child-bearing age, and I would guess you're rather tough for such a small girl."

"Stronger than I look. Anything else?"

"Each of you will have to fight to the death. I've brought my best fighters."

I blinked, trying desperately to find a way to keep

people from dying. "No."

His brows rose. "Excuse me?"

Fawke elbowed me and hissed.

Ignoring him, I stepped out of line. "Give me my sword and a knife. I'll get into that ring with your best fighter. Win or lose, my people are free to stay here or return to the city." I thrust out my hand. "Why lose lives?"

His smile faded, her expression stern again. After staring at my hand for several tense seconds, he gave it a shake. "I'll miss you, little one. You have five minutes to say goodbye to your people."

Nodding, I turned and met the startled faces of my friends. "Well."

"What are you doing?" Fawke grabbed me by the shoulders. "You know I'm the best fighter we have. Why?"

"Because I'm the leader. Don't assume I'll lose, Fawke. You know I'm good and fast with my sword. My size can be an advantage."

"Like I always said, balls as big as buildings, this one." Ezra clapped me on the back. "If you die, I'll kill the one you fought. That's a promise."

"Then I won't lose, because that would mean your death." My chin quivered. "All of you mean too much to me for me to let any of you do this." My gaze locked back on Fawke. "Especially you. Don't you see why I'm doing this?"

"Let me go. Please." His voice shook.

"The deal has been made. Any tips are welcome." I forced a smile.

"Stay low," Ezra said. "Distract with the sword, but jab with the knife."

"Run circles around the guy," Jolt suggested. "Tire him out."

"Don't die." Fawke grabbed me in a hug. "You don't need our ridiculous tips. You need the grace of the Supreme Being."

I couldn't breathe, he held me so tight. My arms snaked around his waist. I took a deep breath of his scent and stepped back. "I can do this." I gave a definitive nod and headed for the arena.

Lloyd held out a sword.

"I want my sword and Fawke's knife." I needed a weapon my hands knew and having something of Fawke's with me would give me strength.

He marched off, scowling, and returned with the items I requested. "Good luck." He stepped into the ring.

I grinned, stopping at a patch of mud. I dipped my fingers in and smeared the mud on my cheeks before climbing under the ropes. The stripes were my badge of leadership. I wouldn't fight without them. "This is fitting. I look forward to killing the one who faked friendship only to kidnap."

"Do your best, little girl." He picked up a sword from the ground. "I'll try to make your death fast."

My heart threatened to beat free as we circled each other. I watched his face, ready for him to make the first move.

He lunged with a yell that raised the hair on my arms. His weapon whooshed through the air.

I ducked and jabbed at his gut, missing, then dropped and rolled out of the way. Leaping to my feet, I swung my sword.

Cheers rose from one side of the ring, cries of

encouragement from the other.

"You go, Crynn!" Jolt yelled.

Not wanting to be distracted, I blocked out all sound other than my breathing and the clanking of our swords as they collided. The contact vibrated up my arms.

Lloyd stood a full head taller and weighed at least eighty pounds more. Survival would be a miracle for me.

His sword skimmed across my mid-section. I hissed and jabbed with my knife, catching him in the upper thigh. Surprise flickered across his face.

"Didn't expect me to draw blood, did you?" I swung my sword over my head.

"Not really." He blocked my swing.

I shot out my leg, tripping him.

He stumbled, but stayed on his feet. His next swing grazed deeper across my ribcage.

I dropped to my knees, striking upward with my sword and slicing through his bicep. He dropped his sword.

Cursing, he moved a few feet away from me, a murderous look in his eyes. He roared and charged.

I rolled out of the way, coming to my feet in one smooth move, sweeping his leg.

He dropped.

I straddled him, my sword at his throat. "It's done." My breath came in gasps.

"Finish him, Miss Dayholt," Jenkins ordered.

I met the resigned gaze of Lloyd, then stepped back, lowering my weapon. "I will not kill him. If we are to fight Soriah, we need every fighter we have." I held out my hand to the fallen man. Blood dripped from my fingers from a cut on my arm I hadn't realized I'd gotten.

Lloyd nodded and accepted my help. "You are a worthy opponent, Miss Dayholt." He bowed.

Together, we faced Jenkins. I prayed my refusing to kill Lloyd wouldn't have dire consequences for my group who now joined us in the ring.

Jenkins shook his head. "You have a point, Little One. I welcome you and yours into our community. Seek medical attention. Tomorrow, you'll all be assigned tasks. No one gets a free ride in Rebel City." He turned and marched away.

"You've got guts," Lloyd said. "Refusing to follow a direct order usually results in death."

"Until he welcomed us in, we weren't citizens. We didn't have to follow his orders."

"Come on." Kira took me by the arm. "I know where the medical building is."

"One minute." I turned to face Fawke, handing him his knife.

He grinned. "You never cease to amaze me." His gaze caressed my face. "You were wonderful."

Now that the adrenaline started to wear off, my limbs trembled, and my cuts felt on fire. "I wasn't so sure a few times." I swayed.

Fawke scooped me into his arms. "Lead the way, Kira. Our little bird needs tending to."

She took my sword from my hand and headed to a small building at the end of the path. Inside, an older woman rolled bandages. Lloyd received treatment opposite the door from another woman.

"Put her here." She motioned to a wooden table. "We'll have her back to normal in no time." She pulled a curtain hung from the ceiling across, blocking me from the others, then started to remove my clothing. "These things have seen better days, young lady. We'll get you something clean to wear and have these washed and repaired."

"Thank you. These rags are a part of me. I don't want to let them go." I sucked in a deep breath as she poured something foul over the cut on my arm.

"This will need stitching. Same with one of the cuts on your mid-section. You're a lucky young lady. The man you fought will require more stitches." She smiled.

A feeling of pleasure washed over me. I might not have drawn first blood, but it sounded as if I'd caused Lloyd to spill more. I closed my eyes and did my best to relax, biting my lip against the pain of the woman's ministrations.

When she'd finished, she handed me a carved wooden cup. "Drink this."

"What is it?"

"Homemade liquor. It'll burn a hole through metal, but it'll numb your pain."

I wrinkled my nose and took a sip, gasping as it burned its way down my throat.

"All of it."

I pinched my nose and upended the cup. Dizziness and numbness washed over me.

The curtain was pulled back and Fawke stood at my side. "Looks like I'll be carrying you back to the hut."

"Yesh." My tongue felt two sizes larger. "I like when you carry me."

He laughed. "That makes two of us." He picked

me up and carried me to my new home.

Inside, he lay me gently on the mattress and sat next to me. "I guess you're no longer my assignment."

"Told you so."

He cupped my face. "I liked watching over you."

"What will you do now?" I could barely keep my eyes open. "Stay or go?"

"Sweetheart, assignment or not, I'm staying with you."

I smiled and closed my eyes.

22

The next morning, a young girl appeared at our shack letting us know that Jenkins wanted to give us our job assignments. I groaned and climbed out of bed, every movement pulling against my stitches.

"I'll help you." Lloyd waited outside, putting his arm around me. "Take tiny steps."

"I appreciate your help, but you're wounded, too."

"These scars make me proud. It isn't every day I find myself beaten by a wisp of a girl." He grinned.

Fawke moved to my other side, sending the older man a sharp look. "I've got her."

"Right." Lloyd stepped away. "I forgot she's your girl, but I'm not looking to step on any toes. I'm old enough to be her father. Heck, maybe even her grandfather."

"Which is why I beat you." I wiggled my eyebrows. "You're an old man."

"Cheeky." He laughed and headed for the center

of the community, leaving my group to follow to where Jenkins waited.

Applause greeted us as people spilled from their homes. Joy bubbled. It seemed like forever since I had a home. Mom would love this place.

"Rebel City welcomes it's new members." Jenkins's voice rose over the noise. "Worthy people joining our ranks. Fighters, young women, strong men. We are blessed indeed."

I smirked. Now, he wants to show how worthy we are. Yesterday, he was willing for one of us to die.

"Crynn, Fawke, I'd like the two of you to be in charge of training warriors once Crynn is fully healed. Kira will join our nurses. The other young women will work in the gardens, the men with our livestock until the fight we all know is coming is upon us. Do you accept these assignments?"

We all nodded. If everyone felt the same as me, they'd do almost anything to live within the safety of this place.

When we were dismissed, the group dispersed except for me and Fawke. He led me to a bench outside my new home and helped me sit.

"How are you feeling?"

"I'm fine. Just sore." I met his concerned gaze. "You're okay with all this? I know how much you wanted to return home."

He sat next to me. "I've done a lot of thinking." He spread his arms behind me on the top of the bench. "When Soriah comes and we win the battle, all of our people will be free. We can bring our mothers here."

"Is winning against Soriah really something we

can do? They have choppers, more weapons than we do." I shook my head. "I don't see us being alive once they arrive."

"Don't bury us yet. It'll be hard to spot us under these trees. Remember, they all think we're dead."

"We could take a small group back to the city and scavenge. Soriah will replace us. We can take their weapons to add to the arsenal here." Ideas formed in my mind. Fawke might be right. We were trained fighters. How many did Soriah actually have within its city walls?

"You'd go back out there?"

"If it meant winning, yes." I watched a little boy hit a wooden ball with a stick. "This life is worth preserving. No more trackers, no more president consumed with making his life easier, no more girls being sent to the entertainment district or eighteen-year-olds fighting Malignants."

"What would we do for a living in this new world you're dreaming of?" He pulled my head onto his shoulder.

"Whatever we want." I closed my eyes and drifted to sleep, not waking until my stomach rumbled.

Kira brought me more of the foul-tasting medicine and a plate with meat and vegetables. "Venison and carrots." She glanced at Fawke. "I should have known you'd be with her. I'll bring another plate."

"Thanks."

"I'll gain ten pounds in no time the way they feed us." I bit into a carrot.

"Good. You're too skinny." He ducked as I

aimed a playful punch at him.

"Ouch." No sudden moves for me. I quickly downed the medicine, then covered the taste with the venison. I picked up another carrot. "We had a small garden back home, but nothing grew like this. I wonder what their secret is."

"Venison manure." Jenkins stopped next to us. "It puts nutrients into the soil. We also have a compost pile. Nothing goes to waste here. Will you excuse us, Fawke? I promise to watch over her and have someone fetch you when we've finished our discussion."

Fawke gave a wary nod, clearly reluctant to leave. Still, he'd been trained to respect authority and marched away without a word.

"That young man would die for you," Jenkins said.

"When I arrived, I was his assignment. He can't seem to let that go."

"Dear girl, he loves you. That's why he hovers."

Was it possible? Now that he wouldn't be leaving me in two years, could we have a future together? I didn't dare hope. The future was still too uncertain. "What did you want to discuss?"

"I must confess to eavesdropping." He didn't look embarrassed in the least. "I agree that we need more weapons. Soriah will come, eventually. If you're serious about heading back to the city to steal from those Soriah sends, then I'm in agreement."

"I am serious." I set my empty plate on the ground. "The problem, though, is that Soriah sent us things the newcomers don't get to choose. Flamethrowers are not in the supply room."

"Guns will do. I've heard a rumor, oh, it's been a long time ago," he waved a dismissive hand, "about an underground armory somewhere in that city. I'd like your group to find out if it exists."

I narrowed my eyes. "Where would we begin?"

"The outskirts. There used to be an army base before Soriah built the wall."

"Why did you send Fawke away to tell me this?"

"It'll be dangerous. I didn't want him to influence your decision."

I widened my eyes. "This isn't a direct order?"

He laughed. "I suppose it is. I value your opinion and wanted to hear your thoughts."

"How will we get supplies?" We'd have no weekly supply drops.

"We'll get supplies to you. Leave a trail of R's on buildings as you go. I'll send men out on a regular basis. I'm asking this of you and yours because you've lived out there. You know what it takes to survive."

I nodded. I'd take my original seven, which included me. "When?"

"As soon as you're physically able." He stood and waved Fawke over. "I'll leave it up to you to let your group know."

Fawke frowned when I told him. "So much for the easy life."

"Someday." I smiled and gazed through the trees surrounding this place. "We'll go back to traveling at night. If a chopper spots us, we'll be finished."

"Spotting that chopper will get us needed supplies."

"Not much. How many can Soriah have sent so

far? One or two?"

"Unless the wheel is rigged to land on black more often." His expression grew grave. "They'll want Stalkers to clear the way for scavengers. I wouldn't put it past them to cheat."

Neither would I. I glanced around the place I wanted to stay. The thought of heading out scared me more than I let Jenkins know. "You'll resume the leadership role. I don't want it. You're more qualified anyway."

He put his arm around me. "Why not lead together? Feel up to hunting up the others and giving them the bad news?"

"Yes. The nap did me good."

He stood and helped me to my feet. "Take a while to heal, okay? I like the food here."

I laughed. "I'll take as long as possible."

Ezra cursed and threw his plate upon hearing the news. "I wanted to find me a woman and settle down."

"The sooner we find the base, the sooner we can return," I said, putting a hand on his arm. "You know that city better than anyone. I'm counting on you."

"I didn't say I wouldn't go." His eyes flashed. "I'll draw up a map of possible sites. It won't be an easy task. The place will have traps. We'll lose people."

I hoped not. "We're only taking seven, but I hope to find others along the way. We can do this."

He nodded, glancing at Fawke. "I know."

We continued on, telling the others of our new mission. Gage pouted and slumped against a wall. "I'd hoped never to go out there again. Why me?"

"Because I want those with me who can fight and won't run screaming at the first sight of a Malignant. Any new Stalkers will be scared out of their minds. We can't let them perish for Soriah's sake." I remember the fear that flooded through me on my first day.

"You didn't say anything about hunting for Stalkers," Fawke said.

"You disagree?"

"No. The more we can take from Cane, the better."

Dante, Moses, and Kira accepted the new assignment, nodding in resignation. "I knew a new life was too good to be true," Kira said. "When do we leave?"

"Once I'm healed."

"Then no more medicine for you." She grinned. "And half rations."

"Let's not go that far." I smiled. "It'll be at least a week or two. Plenty of time for us to gain strength."

"I'm going to spend some time with a girl." Dante stormed away.

"Sounds like a good plan." Moses followed him.

Kira shook her head. "That's all they talk about. I'll make sure we have plenty of medical supplies. The wagons?"

"We'll need them." I'd see about getting back all of our supplies. The more protected we were, the better our chances of survival.

"Let's get you back." Fawke led me home.

I'd miss this little shack and the safety of the trees. The air clear of the stench of Malignants and gas fires. Anger burned in my chest. "I hate this."

"Our sacrifice might be what keeps Rebel City safe." Fawke drew me close. "These people would never be allowed to live if Soriah found them. The children would grow up in orphanages and take their turn someday at the wheel."

"I'm not a hero, Fawke. I'm an eighteen-year-old that wants to grow old with a family around my bed when I die. I want to see my mother again."

"This may be the only chance for that future you dream of."

"Always the voice of reason." I pulled back and stared into his face. "Why not rant and rave against all this like I do?"

"It doesn't serve any purpose. Jenkins said go, so we go. We're soldiers, Crynn. We do as ordered."

I liked that title better than stalker. "Sometimes, I need to throw a pity party. I'll be fine by the time we leave." Already my mind filled with all the things we needed to do. Things to gather.

A familiar sound reached my ears. I lifted my head and stared upward. A chopper flew low over the trees.

"It can't see us." Fawke put a hand on me to stop me from bolting into the house. "The trees are too thick. The shacks are built to blend in, that's why the roofs are covered with dead grass."

"Soriah is looking for us."

"I'm sure they're looking for dead bodies, not live ones. Without our trackers, we're dead."

I wanted to believe him. Instead, my heart lodged in my throat. "We'll be sitting ducks when we leave here."

"Again, they won't know it's us." Concern

crossed his face despite his words.

I'd rather face Malignants than any high-level person from Soriah after finding out we still lived.

23

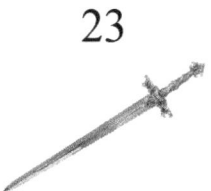

I let myself heal for a week. On the last day, I strolled the path through the center of the community, branding it into my memory. This place already felt more like home than Soriah ever had.

Folks smiled and waved, not worrying over their next meal or their child turning eighteen. Children played with abandon. We hadn't seen another sign of a helicopter, but worry ate at my mind like a flesh-eating bug.

I hunted up my group who were gathered by the wagons. "Is everything here?"

"Yes." Fawke nodded. "Everything they took has been returned. We have chalk to mark our path. Without that, no supplies."

"Weapons?"

"All here. Don't worry, Crynn. I've got this handled." He smiled.

"Medical?" I still had to check.

"Right here." Kira slapped the top of a box.

"More than we had before."

Jenkins must think we'd need the supplies. That thought didn't calm my nerves at all.

"They're having a feast tonight to see us off," Dante said. "I get one more night with my girl."

"I've seen you with a pretty brunette." I smiled, praying he'd see her again after tomorrow. I also prayed we'd find the underground bunker of weapons quickly and be able to return. I didn't relish another month or more in the city.

"Here's the map I've drawn up." Ezra laid a large smooth plank on top of one of the crates. "I used charcoal to draw Xs where I think a bunker could be. I don't think it'll be in the center city, but on the outskirts." He glanced at me. "Which makes us more visible to any choppers flying overhead."

"Unless we see a drop, we travel at night." I studied the map. Three possible places, all miles apart from each other. The base might not have been at any of them.

"Everything ready?" Jenkins approached.

"Looks that way." I turned to greet him.

"Bring back anyone willing to come with you," he said. "Get rid of the others."

"I won't kill anyone just because they don't want to come to Rebel City." I crossed my arms. "But, I will make sure we can trust them before revealing this place."

"Things would be easier, Crynn, if you followed orders as easily as the others." His lips twitched.

Fawke laughed. "I guarantee, you'll never meet anyone more stubborn than this woman."

"I've figured that out."

"They also won't be forced to fight for their life in order to stay." I would not be dissuaded. "If they stick with us long enough to get here, they'll have earned the right." I might be overstepping my boundaries, but fighting to prove your worth was barbaric.

"Relax. I'm not going to argue with you." Jenkins grinned. "See you all at the feast." He continued down the path.

"You're as bossy with him as you were with Sharon," Dante said. "Both very dangerous people to cross."

I shrugged. "I won't be forced into doing something wrong." Satisfied my group had everything under control, I headed back to the house I shared with the other women.

"We'll go with you," Riva said. "All you have to do is ask."

"I appreciate that, but the group needs to be small. The risks are too great." I started packing my few possessions.

"But, you intend on growing your group out there."

"Yes, another reason to start off small. We have to keep from being seen if at all possible." I zipped up my pack. "Enjoy the safety of this place. Your time to fight will come again." And the fight will be more important than any other. We'd be fighting for our future.

As the sky darkened, a large fire was built in the community center. A deer roasted on a pit, filling the air with an aroma so wonderful, my stomach growled. Platters of vegetables and bread made from nuts sat on a wooden table. Every person a part of the community gathered around, smiles gracing their faces.

Jenkins stepped on a sawed-off stump. "People of Rebel City, history is about to be made. This group of warriors will set out in the morning to find the weapons we need to fight Soriah. This is a battle we will win by the grace of the Supreme Being. Keep Crynn and her group in your nightly prayers for their safe return, not only with the weapons, but with additional fighters."

He handed me a metal box. "Three flare guns. We will come if called, but use them sparingly. They're all we have."

"Thank you." We wouldn't be as alone out there as I'd thought. Help would come.

Cheers rose around us as everyone raised their cup of water in a toast.

"Let's feast!" Jenkins cut the first slice of venison and handed it to me. "Come back safely, Little Girl. This community needs you and your group."

I stood as vegetables and bread joined the meat on my plate. Being waited on, hailed, made me uncomfortable. I preferred staying in the background. How my life had changed with the spin of a giant wheel.

After a few restless hours of sleep, I woke and stepped outside. We'd leave in the middle of the night, stopping to camp in the morning before leaving the safety of the trees.

Fawke sat in front of his house. "Couldn't sleep?"

He shook his head. "Knowing we're headed back

out there kept my mind spinning."

"My stomach churned." I sat next to him. "I was foolish thinking I'd never have to leave this place."

He entwined his fingers with mine. "Someday we won't have to."

Unfortunately, today was not that day. I took a deep breath through my nose and exhaled slowly. "Partners, remember? No assignments or leaders."

"I doubt you'll get the others to stop looking at you as their leader." His gaze searched my face. "But, I agree to be your partner. To make decisions with you."

"Then, let's get the others." I headed to the house and woke Gage and Kira. "Ready?"

"No," they said in unison, getting out of bed.

"I could never be ready for this," Gage said.

"Me either." Kira hefted her pack on her shoulder.

We joined the men next to the wagons and put our packs on the ones with supplies. With serious expressions, we sheathed our swords, picked up our guns, and headed out, the wheels of the wagons less noisy on the dead leaves of the forest then they were on the potted streets of the city.

No one spoke. Anxiety hung like a cloud over us. A black bird squawked. I jumped, feeling a lot like I had when I'd jumped from the chopper that first day.

Fawke sent me a quick glance, then focused on the path in front of us. His features looked carved in stone, his brow furrowed.

One of the group behind us, cleared their throat.

At the forest edge, I called a halt. "I'll take first watch." Might as well get back into routine.

"I'll join you." Fawke stayed by my side.

I gazed across the wide meadow at the tops of the buildings rising in the distance. My stomach rebelled, and I vomited in the weeds.

"City of death, here we come," Ezra muttered.

I couldn't think of a better description for what waited ahead.

Don't miss the next book, The Hunt, Coming Soon.

Website at www.cynthiahickey.com

Multi-published and Amazon and ECPA Best-Selling author Cynthia Melton has sold close to a million copies of her works since 2013. She has taught a Continuing Education class at the 2015 American Christian Fiction Writers conference, several small ACFW chapters and RWA chapters, and small writer retreats. She and her husband run the small press, Winged Publications, which includes some of the CBA's best well-known authors. She lives in Arizona and Arkansas, becoming a snowbird, with her husband and one dog. She has ten grandchildren who keep her busy and tell everyone they know that "Nana is a writer".

Connect with me on FaceBook

Twitter

Sign up for my newsletter and receive a free short story

www.cynthiahickey.com

Follow me on Amazon

And Bookbub

Enjoy other books by Cynthia Hickey

Fantasy

Fate of the Faes

Shayna

Deema

Kasdeya